THE
COACHMAN RAT

For Lisbeth, with love

THE
COACHMAN RAT

David Henry Wilson

Carroll & Graf Publishers, Inc
New York

First published in West Germany 1985 under the title Ashmadi

First published in Great Britain 1989
First Carroll & Graf Edition 1989

Carroll & Graf Publishers, Inc.
260 Fifth Avenue
New York
NY 10001

ISBN: 0-88184-508-6

Printed by Richard Clay (The Chaucer Press) Ltd., Suffolk

I

I always knew that somehow I was different. It's true that I looked the same as my brothers and sisters, and to outside eyes no doubt I behaved as they did, but inside I knew that I was me, and there was no-one else in this world that was like me.

I have six brothers and sisters—or had, for they are surely dead now. We lived in the sewers down below Market Street. Of my early days I remember only the constant foraging. My parents showed us how to raid rubbish bins, gnaw through barriers, freeze at the approach of danger, attack when cornered, fight, bite, and eat, always eat. Beware of cats, beware of dogs, and above all beware of man. Men, so they told me, were the scourge of the earth.

"No animal," said my father, "can destroy as man can. He'll slaughter his own kind mercilessly, so expect no mercy for yourself. He'll hunt you, trap you, poison you—but if you're clever you can out-think him and feed off him. Never let him see you. And if he has laid down food for you, run away from it, because it will kill you. Cats and dogs are to be feared when seen, but man is to be feared at all times, visible or invisible. The river flows fast and dangerous, and will swallow you in an instant, but if your choice lies between man and river, then choose the river."

Even then, when I was very young, my imagination was lit up by tales of this monster. What must it be like to have so much power? Should I ever see that power for myself? Could he really kill me? In those days I didn't think that I could even die, and so death was remote. But my father was insistent that death could come to us at any moment, and that man was its likeliest bringer.

One night he failed to come home after a foraging expedition. We wanted to search for him, but my mother stopped us.

"If he can come," she said, "then he will. But if he can't, then it's better for us not to see him."

For nights and days I burned to know what had happened to him. I am ashamed to say that it was not only out of love or concern. No, the feeling that persisted most within me was of curiosity. And at length I had to ask the question that would not leave me in peace:

"Mother, was it man that killed my father?"

She looked at me for quite some time, as if trying to work out the reason for my question, but then she said very softly:

"I don't know. It may have been a cat or a dog. But I think only man would really have been clever enough to catch him."

I should have been afraid, but I wasn't. Whenever we went out hunting, I hoped to see man. And when man did come, my family would force me to run with them, though I wanted to stay. Or perhaps only part of me wanted to stay.

By the time I was full-grown, I was already causing deep concern to my mother, and my brothers and sisters always laughed at me and said I was a dreamer. Foraging, biting, eating, fighting—these things bored me. In the world was a creature that could do a thousand other things, that made me and my fellows seem tiny and insignificant. He had built the towns on which we depended, and in a sense he was a life-giver to us, yet he could take our lives as well, and frequently did. He was awesome. It was his world I wanted to be in.

I grew thin. No-one knew what to do with me. Some said I would grow out of it, others said that it should be knocked out of me, and still others were of the opinion that I should be left alone to survive or die. But I took no notice of them, because they did not understand me. They were them and I was me, and I was different.

For a time I would not even leave the sewer. The sight of man's huge constructions upset me with dissatisfaction. I could never match him or join him, and so I hid away. I should certainly have died if my mother had not fed me on scraps and attended to me. But then I saw for myself that I could not go on in this way. I suppose thoughts were rubbing away at my brain until eventually a new vision broke through and new possibilities became clear.

I rejoined my family, and my mother especially was overjoyed to see me hunting and burrowing and exploring with the rest of them. She thought that I had been ill, and now I was well again. Still strange, perhaps, but well. And I did become well. My coat became sleeker, my body fatter. Outwardly once more I was like all the others—but inwardly, hiding in the walls of my head, I was planning and preparing. I kept asking questions: "How does man trap us, kill us? What are his tricks?" And I was given answers by those more experienced than myself—answers that I stored up. I was told about his poisons and his guns and his traps, above all the traps. Question after question I asked about the traps.

3

And no-one ever suspected why. They all thought I was afraid.

Men make different sorts of traps, and they keep inventing new ones, but they all work according to one basic principle: the victim is enticed with food and is then either killed or caught alive. My father's advice about food laid down was sound: the easier the pickings, the nearer the trap. There is an element of devilry in this principle. But what I had most urgently to learn was the difference in appearance between the killing traps and the catching ones. Until I could distinguish between them, I could not act. Fortunately, there were many venerable souls willing to instruct me, and as my curiosity had become well-known, I was shown plenty of examples. The sight of a fellow-creature broken-backed or messily crushed by a steel spring made me very frightened. These I would avoid at all costs. But the trap that caught its victim alive was quite different: it was a cage, and when the victim went for the bait, a little door would descend so that he would be enclosed on all sides. Once, to the horror of my family and friends, I stayed behind to watch what would happen to one such victim. I hid away and kept very still, and early in the morning (for I made my excursions at night) a man in a white coat came and picked up the trap. I followed him down the street, and saw him pick up two or three more. Then he climbed into a coach, and I could no longer keep pace.

There had been an air of purposefulness about him, which made me distrust him. But clearly he would not have used such a trap unless he had had a specific reason, and this would apply everywhere. The question was: what reason? I should not have wanted to be taken by him, that was sure. It was therefore not enough to know the trap. One must also know the owner of the trap.

I began to forage further and further afield. Sometimes, I would go so far that I couldn't return to the nest before daybreak, and then I would hide away in some hole or dark corner until night fell.

What was I hunting for? All I knew was that when I found it, I would recognize it.

My search lasted for months. Systematically I explored every house in every street, covering every angle of departure from our sewer, and then later from the points that I had already reached. I carefully stored in my memory the location of every trap, and when I found the right trap, I watched for the owner and studied his face and his movements. But in my heart I knew that I should not have to study.

My search came to an end one summer's evening. I found my way into the scullery of a large, old house that was set back from the road behind an iron gate and railings. It looked a grim house, and I entered it without hope of success. Had I not set myself the task of examining every possibility, I should certainly have passed this gloomy place by, but in I went, carefully staying close to the walls and skirting-boards. Traps were usually set in the scullery, and this I found without much trouble. I was struck by the cleanness of the place, and I was even more taken with the trap that I found by the pantry. It was the cage sort, which would trap its victim without harming him.

I was gazing at this trap and thinking how out of character it seemed with the dark hostility of the house, when the scullery door opened. It was at that moment that I saw what I had been looking for.

II

A girl came into the scullery. She was crying, and I watched her sit at the table and put her head in her hands. Now human beings are usually very difficult to tell apart, but I knew at a glance not only that she was female, but also that there was a gentleness about her which is all too rare both in her species and in mine. She was crying very quietly, and I saw some teardrops actually squeeze through her fingers and fall on to the wood of the table. I felt I wanted to comfort her, but how could I?

After a while, she stopped crying, wiped her eyes with a tiny lace handkerchief, and began to peel some vegetables. She had long fair hair that fell round her shoulders, and her eyes were blue, and there was a grace in her movements such as I have often admired in cats but never in humans. She sighed occasionally, but otherwise made no sound as she worked.

Suddenly the scullery door was flung open, and in came two more humans. One of them spoke in a loud harsh voice to the girl, and even I could see the distress on her face when she turned. What these two said to her I don't know, as I understood not a word of human language, but the tone was plainly abusive, and the girl began to cry again. Yet I noticed that when she answered, her voice was soft and with a musical quality.

6

I waited until the girl had gone out, then I quickly left the house and ran all the way home.

When I explained to my mother what I intended to do (and I had to explain it, because I knew that I might possibly never see her again), she was very unhappy.

"You'll be killed!" she said.

"No, I don't think so," I said. "She seems kind and gentle. I don't think she'd kill anything."

"But what do you want to do it for?" asked my mother. "It's madness! You can't join them, you can't be one of them! If you want to observe them, why don't you just hide in a corner and watch?"

"That's not enough!" I said. "I want to know their power. How can I know it unless I give them the chance to show me?"

"To show you how they kill you!" cried my mother. "I can tell you. With a knife, with an axe, with a dog. I thought you'd been cured of this nonsense! Why can't you live a normal life with the rest of us?"

"Listen, mother," I said. "I've seen everything the normal life can offer. Before I was full-grown I'd already experienced every aspect of the normal life, and it's not enough!"

"You never raised a family!" she cried. "You never built a nest of your own!"

"But I've been in a family," I said. "In a happy family. Only look what happened to the father of our family. He disappeared. Why? Do we know? Shall we ever know? His fate is the only mystery that ever penetrated our lives. Perhaps he's in a paradise now. Perhaps he never came back because he found a new world. But if he was killed, that after all was the only other fate that he could head towards. Hunt, forage, bear children, and somehow die."

"What do you want?" she said.

7

"The chance," I said, "the chance for something better."

"There *is* nothing better!" she said.

"That's what I must find out."

I took my leave of her. She watched me go, and although I was sad for her, I was excited as soon as I was out of her view. I had the feeling that I was on the way to a discovery that would give new meaning to the whole of existence. I was going to put myself in the hands of the greatest power on earth. If I was killed . . . but I didn't feel that I was going to die.

Swiftly I reached the grim house behind the gate and railings and found my way to the scullery. Nobody there. But in the corner, beside the pantry, was the trap just as I had left it. There was a little pile of food at the back of it. For a moment I regretted that I should be taken for a creature of foolishness, when the danger was so obvious to the least experienced eye, but that was a mere flash of pride on my part, and I stifled it at once. I stepped into the trap, walked towards the food, and stirred it with my snout, for I was far too excited to eat. At once there was a loud click behind me. I turned, and saw that the door had closed and I was firmly encaged. Now there was no going back.

Nothing happened for a while. I don't know what I had expected—perhaps bells to ring, the girl to rush in, the house to tremble. Not this silence, anyway. I suppose my world was on the verge of an explosion, and I expected the outside world to respond. But when some time had elapsed, and my own limbs began to feel steadier, I actually managed to eat some of the food. Then I nuzzled the cage, to see if any of the bars were loose. It was not that I wanted to escape. I just needed something to do. The bars were not loose, and when I'd tested them all, I was left with the same problem—I had to fill in the time of waiting. What I didn't want to do was think, and the only ways to avoid thinking are to sleep or to act, and I could do neither. I concentrated on the room I was in, staring in turn at the cupboards, table, chairs, sink . . . It had been foolish to enter the trap so soon. I should have gone on exploring until the girl had come—then I could have got myself caught. Why now? Perhaps she wasn't even in the house. Perhaps only those other two humans were there, and one would come in, see me, and . . . madness, madness . . .

What was that? Noises. Yes, clearly, noises in the house. One of those harsh voices calling. *They* were there. Louder now, but not coming nearer, only sounding angrier. Footsteps . . . not towards the scullery, though. Up the stairs. Faintly, the musical voice responding to the harshness . . . two harsh voices, both together. I should have stayed out of the trap. Then I could have seen what was happening. More footsteps, more shouting. Why should those harsh creatures have dominion over the gentle? Back in the sewer, no-one had been able to command his fellow . . . No, that was not true. Some were stronger that others. Some dominated. But none ruled. These two monsters ruled over the gentle girl. Who, then, ruled over the world? Was man himself a divided species?

I could have learnt so much more if I had had patience. I could have lived in this house unseen, and observed human conduct. My mother had said it: hide in a corner and watch. But I had wanted to feel the power. Is it a failing of youth that it wants to take all, never part? Now that I am older, and doubtfully wise, doubtfully cautious, I am inclined to think that such rashness is neither a failing nor a strength. The young are foolish when they fail, and heroic when they succeed. We who are old and cautious may experience neither, and so live emptily.

But at that time I cursed my rashness. I wanted to know what was happening outside, and I had shut myself off from learning. I pushed the bars hard, but they would never give way. Then suddenly from afar a clatter and a rumbling. Jangling shrieks from upstairs, then pattering feet coming down the stairs. That clattering and rumbling, I had heard it before in the streets. Coach and horses. There was a knocking at the front door. More voices. Harsh, harsh. The crash of the door . . . what was happening? Clattering, rumbling, moving away—the coach was leaving. I strained to hear, and the sound died away. Had they all gone? Surely the monsters had, but what of the girl?

"Let her come in now, while they're away!". I said. "Come in, come in!"

A door closed. Someone was there, then. But no-one came to the scullery. Listen, listen, was that the sound of a sob? I couldn't be sure. Strange! Through the door-cracks, it was as if a light was shining—neither a lamp nor a candle would give light like that. I rubbed my eyes. Still there, but moving, and now voices again: the gentle voice, and another just as musical, which I hadn't heard before. Who else was in this house then? Oh, it was so kind this new voice, so soothing and caring and loving. Men were not monsters, not if they talked like this. But perhaps they were like us, some good and some bad, some kind and some cruel. I longed to see the face of the creature with this loving voice. And the light? What could give off light that would penetrate a door and even fill a distant room with its glowing?

Suddenly hurrying steps, coming this way. Rigid with excitement I pressed up against the bars. The door opened, and in came the girl.

"I'm here!" I cried. "Here, in the corner!"

But she took no notice. Instead, she opened the garden door and ran outside. A moment later she was back, carrying a large round fruit in her hand. I'd seen such things before, but had never learned their name. She took the fruit out through the scullery door, and again I heard the loving noise. The scullery door was now open, and evidently the front door was open, too, as the voices came more clearly to my ears. There was a sort of gasp from the girl, as if she had seen something extraordinary. Then the loving voice spoke again, and again the footsteps hurried towards me.

"I'm in the corner!" I cried out to her. "Look, look over here!"

She came close, so close that she almost touched the cage with her bare foot, but she still didn't see me. Instead she opened the pantry door, and disappeared inside. Then out she came with a cage twice the size of mine, and inside were six white mice, shrieking in terror. The girl was speaking softly to them, but they were too stupid or too panic-stricken even to realize that she was talking.

"Let us out!" they screamed. "Save us! Help us!"

I would have shouted at them if she had not rushed out before I could think what to shout. Then once more the voices, once more a gasp of astonishment. Oh something remarkable was happening out there, and I cursed those mice for being a part of it while I was trapped here in my corner longing to be caught up.

The loving voice spoke again. The footsteps came hurrying. This time? Oh come, come, come! And she did. Directly to my corner, directly to my cage. She lifted me and the cage, and for a moment we looked straight into each other's eyes. Such blueness I have seen only in the brightest summer sky. Once more the gentle voice, as

11

if she was trying to soothe me. But I was not afraid. My whole body trembled with excitement, not fear. And she carried me out of the scullery, along the dark corridor. The front door was indeed open, and beyond it was the light that had shone through to the scullery. Whatever lay beyond that door would bring me into the new world I had been seeking.

III

The sight that I saw was breath-taking: a coach of pure gold stood outside the house, and harnessed to it were six pure white horses. Beside the coach, bathed in light, stood a female human. I could not tell if she was young or old; I only knew that she was the most beautiful creature I had ever seen. When she murmured, her voice seemed to wash over me and clean me. As she came towards me I remember thinking that perhaps she would kill me. And I *wanted* to be killed. Dying was the only way in which I could preserve the moment.

But I was not to die. Instead, she touched my head and all at once I felt myself rise and swell. It was as if I was splitting open, and a new me was emerging—a being infinitely greater and more powerful.

"There you are," said the woman of light. "Now you have a coach, and horses, and a coachman to take you to the ball."

12

I looked at her in amazement. She had spoken, and I had understood! I understood their language!

"Thank you, dear Mara," said the girl. "But I can't go in these rags that I'm wearing."

"Of course you can't," said the woman of light. "Here!"

Then she touched the girl, and the rags were at once transformed into silks and jewels.

"From scullery maid to princess," said the woman of light. "And now you can go to the ball."

The girl was indeed a princess. And I? What was I? A man! I looked down at my body, covered in a fine uniform with gold buttons and shiny black boots. I was standing on two legs, I was taller even than the girl, in my hand I held a whip, and in my ears were words, human words, that I could understand and even speak!

"Listen," said the woman of light. "One word of warning. You must leave the ball before midnight. Because at the last stroke of twelve, you'll be a scullery maid again, and all this will be as it was. Don't forget, Amadea!"

"I won't, dear Mara," said the girl. "And thank you, thank you!"

"Robert." The woman of light had turned to me. "Drive Amadea to the ball."

"Yes, ma'am," I said. "But I don't know the way!"

"The horses will take you," she said.

I helped Amadea into the coach, and then vaulted up on to the driving seat. I had seen many coachmen, and I knew what they did. I took the reins in my hand, and cried out to the horses: "Hup! To the ball! Heigh up!"

Away we went. Through the iron gates, down the cobbled street, rumbling and clattering. People turned to look, for we must have been a fine sight: a coach of gold, drawn by six white horses and driven by a splendid coachman in uniform of purple, gold and black. I kept glancing into the shadowy corners, hoping to see my brothers or sisters, but either they were not to be seen, or my human eyes were not sharp enough to spot them. On and on, through street after street, and then suddenly we were racing across a bridge. I had never been here before. Below us was the river that my father had feared, and even in this half light I could see the glint of the fast-flowing water. Then we were galloping along a broad, tree-lined avenue, and into sight came the grandest house imaginable, with white walls and towers, and a great flight of stone steps that led to a golden gate. "The Prince's Palace!" I murmured to myself.

Outside the palace were dozens and dozens of coaches, and from inside came the sound of music—rhythmic and gay, telling your feet to dance.

We stopped at the foot of the steps, and two servants ran to the door of our coach to help Amadea down. I watched her descend, gracefully from the step to the ground, and then she came to the front of the coach and looked at me. Once more I saw the blue of her eyes, which were shining with excitement.

"Thank you, Robert," she said. "Will you wait for me?"

"Yes, ma'am," I said.

She smiled at me, and then up the steps she went, fairly dancing, and in through the golden door.

"Take the coach over there, will you?" said one of the servants, pointing to a space between two other coaches.

I drove into the gap and parked.

"Some coach you've got there!" said a deep gruff voice. I looked across at the owner of the voice—a huge, red-faced man in the driving-seat of the coach on my right. "Jack's the name," he said. "Never seen a coach like that—not even the Prince's is like that."

"No, it's a special coach," I said.

14

"Haven't seen it or you before," said Jack.

"No, we're from out of town," I said.

"Got a name, have you?"

"Robert."

"Pleased to meet you, Robert."

He leaned across and we shook hands.

"No," he said, "they don't make coaches like that round here. Mind if I have a look?"

"Not at all," I said.

Jack got down, and so did I, then I watched as he examined my coach. Every so often he would gasp.

"Never seen anything like that before!" he said. "Hey, Bill, Harry, come and have a look at this!"

Before long there was a crowd of coachmen clustered round my coach.

"Looks like solid gold," one of them said.

"Can't be," said another. "*Is* it solid gold?"

"No," I said. "No, it's not solid gold."

"Clever," said the first. "You'd really think it was."

I don't know why I said it wasn't. Perhaps I was still afraid of these men, and I didn't want them to pay so much attention.

"Tell you something else," said Jack. "That mistress of yours, she's the best-looking dame I've seen here all evening. Who is she?"

"She's a princess," I said.

"I can see that," said Jack. "But where's she from?"

"A long way away," I said. "You wouldn't know our town."

"Here, lads, let's have a drink!" said a jolly-looking coachman waving a bottle in the air. This seemed to draw attention away from me and my coach, and I was grateful.

"You as well," said the jolly man, and the bottle was passed to me. The liquid was sharp and warm, and I felt it go all the way down into my stomach. It had a strange effect on me, because all at once I no longer felt afraid. Instead, I had a feeling of well-being.

The music was still coming loud and clear into the evening air, and the urge to dance became stronger.

"Here, lads," I cried, "they're all having a ball in there, so why don't we have one out here?"

"Good idea!" came a chorus of voices, and before I really knew what I was doing, I had started to dance. The others didn't join in at first. They just watched me, and clapped in rhythm to the music and to my movements. There was no plan to what I was doing, I simply followed my feet, and they took me between coaches, round coaches, over coaches, up the steps, down the steps, always in rhythm, always light and leaping. When the music finished, I finished, and the whole crowd cheered.

"Have another drink!" cried the jolly man, and I did. Then the music started up again, and everybody danced. Sometimes we danced alone, sometimes with each other. Some women came from the Palace to join in—not the great ladies of course, but some of the maidservants who had finished their work. There was a lot of laughter, and I remember thinking that women's laughter was as beautiful as music.

After a while, the music stopped altogether, and some servants came down the steps with trays full of food and drink for us. Then we sat round talking and laughing. The coachman called Jack told us a story about how he had once lost his way and had to sleep on some hay.

"When I woke up in the morning," he said, "I was sleeping on the hard ground. There wasn't a wisp of hay in sight. But the horses were still there, and my, did they look fat!"

16

We all roared with laughter, and more stories were told, more drink was drunk, and the mood grew merrier and merrier.

"Have you got a story for us, Robert?" asked the jolly man.

"Yes, I'll tell you a story," I said. "But let's have another drink first."

"Wet your whistle, eh?" said Jack.

The more I drank, the lighter I seemed to become, and the easier it was to talk.

"I'll tell you a story about a friend of mine," I said. "He wasn't a man at all, this friend of mine. He was a rat."

"A rat!" they shouted, and howled with laughter.

"Now this rat," I said, "had one ambition in life, which was to be a coachman. And he spent all his time hunting around to find somebody who'd be able to change him. What he really wanted, you see, was a woman of light."

"A light woman!" they howled, and hooted with laughter.

"Well eventually," I continued, "he found a woman of light . . ."

"Light woman!" they howled again and hooted again.

". . . who did all the necessary, and changed him into a coachman. She also changed a pumpkin into a golden coach, and six white mice into six white horses. And here they are, and here I am!"

They fairly doubled up with laughter, and the jolly man slapped me on the shoulder and said it was the funniest story he'd heard in years. I found it difficult to get my thoughts straight. I hadn't meant the story to be funny, and I couldn't see *why* it was funny, and yet here they all were, shrieking with laughter and telling me what a funny fellow I was.

"Actually, it's the truth!" I said to the jolly man, but he only shrieked louder.

"Have another drink," he said. "You're the best story-teller I've heard for a long time. Drink up!"

After another drink, I stopped trying to puzzle out why they had laughed, and I found myself laughing just as loudly as them. Then the music began again, and so did the dancing. I felt wonderfully warm inside, and the people around me seemed like friends that I had known all my life. There were no monsters among them. This was one large family linked together through enjoyment of the sort I had never dreamed of. Even drinking was a pleasure. Had we of the sewer ever eaten or drunk for pleasure? Had we ever danced, ever laughed? Had life ever meant anything more than maintaining our existence?

I danced with a serving-girl. We had our arms round each other and were laughing for no reason other than enjoyment. She had none of the sweet gentleness of Amadea, and none of the loving peace of the woman of light, but I had an affinity with her. How can I describe it? As if we were from the same world.

The music stopped briefly, and she raised her face up close to mine. Our lips met, and I closed my eyes to feel her the more intensely. Such softness, round-ness, ripeness. Like this, one could float into another being.

The music started again, and we danced again.

"Go easy, Robert!" called big Jack. "Take the girls' feet and take their lips, but leave them their hearts!"

There was more laughter, and I laughed too and held the girl even closer. I had found the world I wanted.

And then the bell struck.

IV

"**M**idnight," said the girl.

At first the word meant nothing to me, but then as the bell went on chiming, I dimly remembered the voice of the woman of light. Hadn't she warned Amadea to leave the ball before midnight?

"You'll be a scullery maid again!" I said aloud, to the consternation of the maid I was dancing with.

I never even said goodbye to her. I raced up the stone steps towards the golden door just as the last stroke sounded. Towards me came Amadea, and suddenly . . . I was below the level of the next step. She was towering over me, and then she was gone, running away from the Palace and the coaches, down along the tree-lined avenue. At the foot of the steps I heard someone squeal: "Look at the mice!" and there was a surge in the crowd around where my coach had been. Someone else shouted: "It's a pumpkin!" There was a sudden flurry of activity, and I saw many arms rise and fall.

"Kill the little pests!" came the unmistakable gruff voice of big Jack.

What would they do to me if they found me? I cowered against the step, but there were servants all around, and the step was lit by the thousand torches all the way up the sides. Should I stay, should I run? At least if I ran, I might have a chance.

"Look, up there, on that step! A rat!"

Someone down below had seen me. I ran in the only direction possible—up through the golden door. I found myself in a huge hall full of men and women, beautifully dressed, holding each other, smiling . . . Wasn't this my world?

"Oh, a rat!" screamed one of the beautifully dressed women.

The people scattered, and servants came up the steps behind me. I could not go forward or back.

"Kill it!" shouted a harsh voice.

Attack when cornered, my father had said. I must attack or be killed. Attack, attack.

I turned and ran towards the golden door. A leg struck at me, but I was too quick. I leapt at the standing leg and bit it. There was a cry of pain, and the man fell down, hampering his fellows. This gave me just the fraction of time that I needed to be out and away. Down the steps I raced, and off into the night, along the tree-lined avenue, and across the bridge that spanned the fast-flowing river. As I ran, I wondered briefly if I would see Amadea.

There had been a few shouts behind me, but very soon I knew I was clear. There was no sign of Amadea, and the streets of the town were deserted. Whoever was not at the Prince's ball was asleep. All I wanted to do was get home and tell my mother that I was safe and that I had seen another world. But I was too far away to reach home that night, and so when dawn began to break, I hid inside a ruined wall and slept.

Of the rest of my homeward journey there is nothing to relate. It was not long before I found an area of the town that I knew, and from there it was easy to trace the route back to my sewer. When I got there, my brothers and sisters were all out foraging, but my mother was at home, and in my excitement I began at once to tell her my story:

"Mother, mother!" I cried. "I've had the most unbelievable experience! I was turned into a coachman! I went to the house I told you of, and there I met Amadea and a woman of light, who made me into a man! I had a uniform, and I drove six. . . ."

I broke off. There was a look in my mother's eyes that made me into a total stranger.

"Do you hear me, mother?" I cried.

Then she spoke. At least she opened her mouth, and I could see that she was speaking. But the sound that came out was just a high-pitched squeak.

"What are you saying?" I shouted.

But there were no words from her—only this interminable squeak. Perhaps she was ill, or perhaps it was just the shock of seeing me again when she thought I had been killed. I decided to wait till my brothers and sisters returned—at least they would be able to tell me what was wrong with her.

They did return eventually, but before I could even speak to them, my mother had started again with her high-pitched whining. And they responded—with the same sounds! Only then did I realize what had happened. I no longer spoke their language! I had lost my human form, but not my human words! I had lost the means of communicating with my own kind!

They drove me out of the nest and out of the sewer. Can I blame them? I had always been different from them, but still recognizably one of their species. Now I spoke like their most dreaded enemy. How could they possibly let me stay in their midst?

I hid in a crevice and wrestled with my situation. One solution stood out above all others. I could hunt for a killing trap and put an end to myself. It would be over in a moment—the spring would break my back and I would feel nothing more. Whereas living would bring unlimited pain.

Yet I *wanted* to live. I wanted to be a coachman, and if I let myself be killed, that would be an end to the whole dream. I had set out to find a new world, and now that I had found it and lost it, surely I should search for it again. Once found is hope for future findings. Never to have found is cause for despair. That world existed, and that world had contained me once. Could it not contain me again?

The woman of light held the key. She had the power to transform me, and if I could find her, then I could find my way back to the being I had once been. But where would she be? The obvious place to look was Amadea's house. At least I should lose nothing by going there, and if ultimately my search were to prove fruitless, then there would always be the killing traps to turn to.

I set out for Amadea's house. It was easy enough to find, and easy enough to enter. Once more I made my way to the scullery, but Amadea was not there. In the distance I could hear voices, and so I crept up the stairs till I found the room the voices came from. Two I recognized at once—the harsh tones of the women who had commanded Amadea. The third was equally harsh, but older. Perhaps their mother. The door was slightly ajar and I listened in to the conversation.

"What do you mean you never recognized her?" the mother was saying.

"How could we, in all that finery?"

"If we'd only known in advance, you could have cut your toes off and the shoe would have fitted you."

"I'd never have got it on, mother, even if I *had* cut my toes off."

"It's absurd, two fine girls like you passed over. And all

because of a small foot. What basis is that for a marriage? I don't know what the world's coming to."

"He fell in love with her, mother, that's all there is to it. We had our chance, but the shoe didn't fit in more senses than one."

"Very philosophical, I'm sure. And now what am I to do with you?"

"No more and no less than you've done before, mother."

"Don't you start being clever with me, my girl. There aren't all that many golden futures in this town."

I understood the words of this conversation, but the meaning escaped me completely. Evidently there were human customs I knew nothing of, and the events they were discussing clearly had nothing to do with me or with the whereabouts of the woman of light. My only hope now was that they would mention the whereabouts of Amadea, but the mother said she wanted a cup of tea, and one of the sisters came to the door. I barely had time to scurry into the next room before she had come out into the passage.

The sister went downstairs to the kitchen, and that was the strongest indication so far that Amadea was not in the house. Otherwise, the sister would certainly have shouted for her. With hindsight, of course, I realize that I should have gathered more from the conversation than I actually did, but at the time it was simply confusing and seemingly irrelevant. I listened for a while longer but the talk was still of shoes and marriage and blank futures—none of which meant anything to me. As soon as it was safe, I ran down the stairs and left the house. My plan now was to hide near the front door and stay there till Amadea returned.

I waited and watched all through the night and all through the next day. People came and went, but of

Amadea there was never a sign. I tried to think back over the events of that midnight outside the Palace. I had seen her running down the steps, but I had seen so little else of what had happened to her. Could it be that men had chased her, caught her, killed her? Had not my father said that men killed one another mercilessly? They had been such good companions to me that I had forgotten their reputation, but with my own eyes I had seen the slaughter of the mice. And had not the sisters used Amadea like some inferior creature? When Amadea had run down the steps, she had been in her kitchen rags. Perhaps the people at the Palace had realized that she was an outsider, just as the mice had been, and I myself. Perhaps it was the human custom to kill outsiders.

I would have to ask someone what had happened. But if I revealed myself, I would also be open to slaughter. Would it be possible to ask without revealing myself? Perhaps in the darkness of night I would find the chance.

When dusk had fallen, I wandered out into the streets. There were never many people around after dark, which was why we had always preferred to forage at night. But I remembered that occasionally we would see men and hide from them, and this was my hope now.

I had walked the streets for hours when I came to a park. I had never paid much attention to such places in the past, because men neither worked nor lived there, and so would not set traps. But the thought now occurred to me that perhaps men might rest there, even in the night. I squeezed through the railings, and ran over the grass. Before long, I saw what I had hoped to see— a man lying stretched out on a bench. Near the bench was a tree, and I placed myself behind the tree, so that he would not be able to tell where I was.

"Excuse me!" I called.

The man stirred.

"Sorry to disturb you," I said. "I wonder if you can give me some information."

The man sat up. "Information?" he said. "Where are you?"

"Does the name Amadea mean anything to you?" I asked.

"Where are you?" said the man again, and I could see even in the dark that he was peering round him.

"I'm over here," I said. "It doesn't matter where. I just wanted to know what had happened to Amadea."

"Who's Amadea?" asked the man.

"If you haven't heard of Amadea," I said, "perhaps you've heard of the woman of light."

"Woman of light!" cried the man. "You're having me on, aren't you? Come on, where are you? Show yourself!"

He stood up.

"Give us a clue," he said.

"What do you mean?" I asked.

He came towards the tree.

"You're up in the tree, ain't you?" he said. "Come on down, so I can see you."

Obviously I was not going to learn anything from him. His one concern was to find me, and although I could sympathize with him over the frustration of seeking and not finding, I had no intention of giving him what he wanted. I had just resolved to run away when he spoke again:

"This Amadea of yours, and the woman of light —I do know where they are, as a matter of fact. Only if you want to know, you'll have to show yourself. I'm not giving away information like that to someone I can't see. Right?"

I did not run away.

"I can't show myself to you," I said. "If I do, you won't believe what you see."

"No see, no information," said the man. "Take it or leave it."

He returned to his bench, and put his feet up. I came out from behind the tree, still uncertain what to do. I knew I couldn't trust him, but was there anyone I could trust? If he had the information, I must try to get it from him.

"I'm over here," I said, "by the tree."

He turned and looked over the back of his bench.

"Can't see you," he said. "You'll have to come closer."

I did. I went and stood behind the bench, so that he would be able to look down at me without being able to reach me.

"I'm down here," I said.

"Well I'm damned!" he said. "I'll be damned. A bloody rat!"

He turned his head away, and knocked it with his hand. I had seen his face for the first time—lined and shaggy with a thick beard. He was wearing a hat, so that it was difficult to see his eyes. Through the bars of the bench I could see that his clothes were ragged and torn.

"Alc'ol must be getting to me brain!" he said. "Bloody rats don't talk!"

He looked down at me again.

"Strewth!" he said.

"I can talk," I said. "I was once a coachman. I'm trying to find the woman of light so that she can make me a coachman again."

"A talking rat!" he said. "Now I've seen everything."

"You told me you knew where they were," I persisted. "Now I've shown myself to you, please give me the information."

26

The man took off his hat. He had a shock of tangled hair which he now ruffled with his hand.

"That's right," he said. "Amadea and the woman of light. As a matter of fact, I know them very well. Now, if you just look over there, in the direction of the road, you'll see a big house with lights in the windows. See it?"

I followed the direction in which he was pointing, and suddenly everything went completely dark. It was as if I had been cut off from the whole world. He had dropped his hat on me.

V

Before I could even begin to burrow or gnaw, the man was on top of me, and he had swept me up inside the hat, gripping me so tightly that I could hardly breathe.

"Now then," he said, "let's have a good look at you."

Carefully, he folded back the brim of the hat until he had uncovered my head, but still he gripped me in such a way that I could not turn enough to bite him.

"You're breaking my ribs," I gasped.

"You'll survive," he said. "A talking bloody rat. Big fellow, too, ain't you, strong . . . Keep still! Or I'll break your bloody neck. Where'd you learn to talk, eh?"

"I told you," I said, "I was a coachman."

"Coachman, eh? A coachman rat. This is my lucky day, you know that? You've dropped from heaven, you have. You and me together, coachman rat, can make a fortune. Play my cards right, and I'll be a rich man. Fred Biggs and his talking rat. You got a name, coachman?"

"Robert," I said. "Please let me go."

"Let you go, let go a fortune. No, no, Robert, you and me's going into business together. Bobby, that's what I'll call you. Fred Biggs and Bobby. We'll be world famous. Only I can't hold you like this for ever more. No, you come with me."

Still holding me painfully rigid, he set off across the park and out into the street. I kept calling to him to let me go, but he took no notice at all. I was as much a prisoner in his hands as I had been in Amadea's trap, but this time I had been caught involuntarily and I was badly frightened. I kept thinking of my father's warnings and my mother's distress. The human world was not just coaches and music and dancing. There were monsters at large, and now I had stupidly put myself in the power of one of them. It was no use trying to reason with myself that I had earlier been prepared to die rather than never know the human world. Fear does not yield to reason.

He took me into a yard where there were piles of boxes that contained various sorts of fruit and vegetables, as I could see between the slats. At his approach, there was the sound of scurrying feet which I recognised as belonging to my own kind. But Fred Biggs paid no attention to them. Instead, he bent down between two stacks of crates, and held me against the opening of what I at once recognized as a non-killing trap.

"Now get in there!" he hissed.

He relaxed his grip in such a way that I had no room to turn but must either stay still or go forward into the trap.

"Go on!" he said, and pushed my hind-quarters with his free hand. I went forward and then tried to turn round and run out, but he was too quick for me, and slammed the door down.

"Got you!" he said.

Then he picked up the cage and set off down the street again. I pushed at the door, and I gnawed at the bars, but nothing gave way. I called out once more that he should let me go, but the appeal was futile. It was not until we had returned to his park bench that he spoke to me again.

"Now then, Bobby," he said, "this is what we're going to do. I'm going to look after you, like you was my own son. I'll give you whatever's your favourite food, I'll keep you nice and clean, I'll even give you velvet cushions to lie on and a toy coach to play with, if that's what you want. And in return for my kind-heartedness, you will talk whenever I tell you to. Right? That's all you have to do, just talk. How's that for an agreement?"

"Why are you doing this?" I asked. "Why are you keeping me prisoner?"

"Money!" he said. "What else would I do it for?"

"What *is* money?" I asked.

"Ah," he said, "they didn't teach you that when you were a coachman, then? Money, my friend, is the answer to all our problems. Money means food, money means clothes, money means a roof over your head and a chair to sit in and a bed to sleep in. Money means respect. The more money you have, the more people will tip their caps to you. Without money I'm a tramp, with money I'm Mister Biggs, and with a lot of money, I'm 'sir'. One day, 'Your Lordship'. Money, my little friend, is the difference between starving, living, and living in luxury. If that woman of light of yours ever grants you a wish, then wish for money. Because with money, you'll get the rest of your wishes without so much as a wand-wave."

"Will money get me my freedom?" I asked.

"My little friend," he replied. "If you were able to give me a thousand pounds, I'd open this door for you right now. But you can't, so I won't."

"Will you let me go when you've got enough money?"

"I might do. But then again I might not. You see, I don't know if I shall *ever* have enough money. What I think is enough now might not be enough then. Don't pin your hopes on anything, Bobby. No expectations means no disappointments."

By now it was daybreak. One or two people were already walking through the park, but they hurried past Mister Biggs as if they hadn't seen him. He called out to one man: "Spare a penny, mister?" but the man merely walked faster. "See what I mean?" Mister Biggs whispered to me. "If you're poor, they don't want to know you."

He took out a paper bag in which there was some bread and cheese. He broke off a piece and pushed it through the bars for me, then he ate the rest himself.

"Now then," he said when he had finished, "it's the market-place for us. And when I tell you to talk, talk. If you don't, you'll get a taste o' this."

From his pocket he pulled a knife, and he pushed it through the bars till it was close to my eye.

"We do it friendly," he said, "or we do it nasty. But we do it, right?"

"What am I supposed to say?" I asked.

"Anything you like," he said. "So long as you talk."

We set off for the market-place. I wondered if I should see my family there, but it turned out to be a different place altogether, much bigger than the one we had lived under. By the time we arrived, it was already crowded, and if I had not been in my cage high above the ground, I should certainly have been trampled to death.

Mister Biggs got hold of two wooden crates, which he stacked one on the other, and he placed me on top. Then he stood in front of me and began to shout in a very loud voice:

"Roll up, roll up! Come and listen to the talking rat! A penny a time! The only talking rat in the world!"

A few people stopped. Eventually a man gave Mister Biggs a penny and was allowed to approach my cage.

"Talk, Bobby!" said Mister Biggs.

I had already worked out exactly what I was going to say.

"Please," I said, "if you know where the woman of light is, tell her to come and save me."

"Bless my soul!" said the man who had paid a penny. "It really does talk! How's it done?"

"Otherwise, tell Amadea . . .."

"Very clever," said the man. "The voice really seems to come from the rat."

"Of course it does!" I said.

"That's enough, Bobby," said Mister Biggs. "If they want to hear more, they'll have to pay more."

And pay more they did. The pennies seemed to flood in all day long as people queued to hear the talking rat. Most of them thought it was a trick, and several even examined the boxes on which I was standing. But Mister Biggs never let them stay long, and no-one ever had the time to answer my questions about the woman of light and Amadea. Only once did a woman begin to answer:

"Amadea? Isn't that the name of the girl the Prince . . ."

But Mister Biggs was already ushering her away so that the next customer could come and listen.

It was Mister Biggs who finally told me the answer. It was evening, and people had left the market. He sat down on the box beside me, and emptied out his hat which was full of coins. Then he counted up the money.

"One pound four shillings and threepence!" he said. "What a day! We're going to be rich, Bobby!"

"Is that a lot of money?" I asked.

"I'll say it's a lot! And that's just the first day! Now you and me, my boy, we're going to have something to eat, and you can choose whatever you like. Incidentally, I've got some news for you. That Amadea you were talking about. She really exists."

"I know she does," I said. "You told me you knew where she was!"

"Well, that was so I could bring you out in the open. Tactics, like. But I heard some people talking about her. You'll never guess who she is."

"Tell me, please."

"She's the girl that's going to marry the Prince, that's who she is. So you've been moving in high circles, me lad. Come on now, let's go and have supper."

"Where will she be then?" I asked.

"She'll be in the Palace, won't she? But I don't think you and me'll be going there, not for a while anyway. Not till we've made our fortune."

"Can't you take me there so that I can speak to her?" I asked.

"You must be joking, mate!" he said. "They'd never let me within smelling distance. Besides, you and me we've got too much work to do to go off visiting princesses. Supper!"

We ate well that night, as we did every night after Mister Biggs had counted his money. Day after day we went to the market or to some busy street or fairground, and day after day I was made to talk, to answer questions, to 'perform'.

There were two occasions, however, when this routine was broken. On the first, we found ourselves mingling with a great crowd in the market-place. A huge pile of sticks and planks and branches had been erected in the middle of the square, and soon a horse-drawn cart arrived with several men and a woman who was dressed all in black. Her hair was loose around her shoulders and she was fighting with the men and screaming all the time.

"Burn her! Burn her!" shouted the people around, and Mister Biggs joined the chorus.

The men tied the woman to a high pole that protruded from the heap of wood, and then they stepped down.

"Burn her! Burn her!" howled the crowd.

"Burn the witch!" shouted Mister Biggs. "Roast her to hell."

The men produced torches, and set the wood alight. I watched with horror as the fire swept upwards, creaking and crackling, darting towards the woman, who never ceased screaming.

"Why are they doing this to her?" I asked Mister Biggs.

"Why?" he said. "Because she's evil, that's why. Burn, witch, burn!"

The flames danced all around her, and at last her jerking body slumped. Soon it had disappeared completely behind the wall of fire, and the crowd cheered loudly.

It was the most horrible sight I had ever seen.

The other break in our work was for a very different reason. On that morning Mister Biggs announced that I was in for a special treat.

"Big day today," he said. "No-one'll want to hear your voice. But you're going to see an old friend of yours."

The streets were alive with people, and I had never seen so much colour and gaiety. Bright cloths hung everywhere and people wore their merriest clothes.

"What's happening?" I asked.

"You'll see," he said.

We took our place in a deep line of people, and watched as a group of children danced by, playing pipes. Mister Biggs held my cage up high so that I could see everything that was going on. Horses came by, with riders in shining uniforms, and then more dancers, more music, more children. In the distance I could hear loud cheering, and it seemed to be coming nearer and nearer. Horses, music, dancers . . . and then a rumbling clatter.

"You watch this!" cried Mister Biggs, as the cheers echoed all around us.

And what I saw was six horses, three white and three black, drawing a carriage of gold and silver. Sitting in the carriage, waving and smiling happily, were a handsome young man and a beautiful girl. And I knew at once that the girl was Amadea.

VI

"Married now, you see," said Mister Biggs that evening, as we sat in the park and ate our supper. "Done all right for herself, your Amadea. She wouldn't want to see the likes of you and me now, would she."

"But I have to see her!" I said. "She's the only one who can tell me where to find the woman of light!"

"Well Bobby, my old son," he said. "If there is a woman of light, there's a *lot* of people'd like to find her! But I reckon the nearest you and me'll ever get to a woman of light is each other, and that's how it's going to stay. Let's have a little drink."

Mister Biggs had taken to having a lot of little drinks, and as the weeks went by, he drank more and more. Sometimes the drink made him happy, sometimes irritable, and sometimes sleepy. There were days when we didn't work at all, and days when he forgot to feed me. I had become very thin, and I was indeed in despair of ever being free and ever finding the goal I had set myself. But my life was due to undergo yet another change.

Mister Biggs had spent all his money, and so once more he took me to the market, just as he had done on that first day. He set me up on two boxes, as he always did, and began to shout for pennies. Everything proceeded as normal, and perhaps half of the day had gone by when a carriage came through the market-place and stopped near us. A man climbed out of it, and I could see at once that he was different from everyone else. He was grey-haired, with round glasses on the end of his nose and a walking stick in his hand. People actually made way for him as he approached us.

"Are you the man with the talking rat?" he asked Mister Biggs.

"That is correct, sir," said Mister Biggs. "The only talking rat in Christendom, and you can talk to him for a penny, sir."

"Here's a shilling," said the gentleman. "I should have quite a conversation for that."

"Yes, sir, thank you, sir," said Mister Biggs. "You can talk as long as you like for that, sir."

The gentleman bent over my cage.

"Is is true you can talk?" he said to me.

"Yes, sir," I replied.

"Where did you learn?"

"I trained him, sir," interrupted Mister Biggs. "I taught him everything he knows."

"Now my good fellow," said the gentleman. "I've paid a shilling for this conversation, but with the rat, not with you. And I want you to stand far enough away not to hear what we're saying, you understand? I must be sure there's no trickery here."

Mister Biggs meekly withdrew, mumbling only that there was no trickery, and then the gentleman returned his attention to me.

"Say something," he commanded.

"What do you want me to say, sir?" I asked, and noticed that he swiftly glanced towards Mister Biggs.

"The voice is certainly from the cage," he said. "Or perhaps beneath."

He stooped to examine the boxes, and then had some difficulty straightening up again.

"Nothing there," he said, turning again towards Mister Biggs. "I shall give you five pounds if you'll tell me how it's done."

"I don't know, sir. I wish I did."

"Ten pounds."

"Strewth, sir, I'd tell you if I could."

"Do you swear there's no trickery here?"

"If there was, sir, I'd tell you for five pounds, let alone ten."

"You didn't train him yourself?"

"No, sir, he was like this when I caught him."

"Who trained yoú to speak?" the gentleman asked me directly.

"Sir," I replied, "I was the coachman who drove the

Princess Amadea to the ball. It was the woman of light who changed me into a coachman, but then I changed back again into my present form."

"You mustn't lie to me," said the gentleman.

"Sir, I'm not lying!"

"Remarkable!" said the gentleman. "Did your owner train you?"

"No, sir," I said. "I was made into a man by the woman of light."

The gentleman looked at me for a long time, as if trying to decide something about me. Then he said:

"If I took you away from your owner, would you still be able to talk?"

"Yes, sir," I said. "He's not my owner. He caught me and trapped me by trickery."

The gentleman turned abruptly away and walked across to Mister Biggs. There followed a discussion which I was unable to hear, but there was a good deal of head-shaking and hand-waving. At length they seemed to agree, and the gentleman took a small bag from his coat pocket, and counted out some gold coins which he gave to Mister Biggs. Then they shook hands.

Mister Biggs came across to me.

"I've sold you," he said. "I'm a rich man. You brought me luck, you did. So you make sure you behave yourself and talk. Otherwise he's going to come for his money back."

He picked up the cage with me in it, and handed us over to the gentleman, who had now climbed back into his carriage.

"Here you are, sir," he said. "And good luck to you both."

"Drive on, Morton!" the gentleman called to his coachman, and away we went. I caught one last glimpse of Mister Biggs, who was counting the gold coins, but then he disappeared from my view.

"Now then," said the gentleman, "we must get to know each other. My name is Dr. Richter, and I'm a scientist. You know what a scientist is?"

"No, sir," I said.

"A scientist," he said, "is a person who observes, collects, and systematizes facts, in an effort to understand the nature of the world. We form and test theories that are based on the facts. And we hope to achieve truth. You understand?"

"I think so," I said. "We do the same when we go foraging."

"There are differences," said Dr. Richter, "but we needn't go into them. Do you have a name?"

"I was called Robert when I was a coachman, but Mister Biggs called me Bobby."

"Robert will do nicely. Now when we get home, I'm going to ask you a lot of questions, and I shall expect you to answer truthfully. I want no lies, you understand? Science cannot advance through lies."

I assured him that I would tell him whatever he wanted to know, and then I asked if he would set me free when I'd told him everything.

"That's something I can't promise," he said. "You may be too valuable to set free. We shall see."

Dr. Richter's house was large and light—quite different from Amadea's. A servant opened the door for us, and the moment we entered, we were greeted by a very fat red-faced woman.

"Goodness me, Dr. Richter," she exclaimed, "what *have* you got there?"

"As you can see, Mrs. Dumpling, it's a rat."

"Oh, dear."

"Not an ordinary rat, though, Mrs. Dumpling. This

rat is unique, and is to be treated with the utmost respect. I shall want a proper cage for him, with plenty of room and comforts. And he's to be fed regularly, on whatever he asks for."

"Asks for, Dr. Richter?" said the fat lady in surprise.

"Exactly, Mrs. Dumpling," said Dr. Richter. "You see, he's a *talking* rat."

"Well I never!" said Mrs. Dumpling. "What *will* they think of next!"

I was duly cleaned and fed and installed in a large and very comfortable cage. But never for one moment was I given the chance to get free. The new cage was as solid as the old, and my hopes of escaping to see Amadea were as slim as ever.

I was left to settle in on that first evening, but the very next day Dr. Richter began his questioning. He sat beside the cage with a pencil and notebook in hand, but there were difficulties right from the start.

"Now the first thing I want to find out," he said, "is exactly how you learnt to speak our language. This story of being a coachman and . . . that's obviously absurd. What is the truth?"

"That *is* the truth, sir," I said.

"No, no," he said, "you mustn't lie!"

I assured him yet again that I was not lying, and at his request I told him my whole story right up to that moment. He sat silently, taking notes all the time, but when at last I had finished, he shook his head.

"There *are* no women of light," he said. "There's no such thing as magic. What people take to be magic is either trickery or has some logical physical explanation. Science deals with facts, Robert. Your talking is a fact, but your explanation is—to be blunt—hocus-pocus."

"I swear to you it's true!" I cried. "Every word of it is true."

He frowned, and reflected for minutes on end. Then he looked straight at me.

"If you don't change your story," he said, very severely, "I shall have you killed. I have no time for fairly-tales."

"Sir," I said, "I could tell you lies in order to save my life, but you didn't want to hear lies. My story is the truth, and I shan't tell you another."

He continued to gaze at me, and for a moment I had a strange feeling akin to hope that he would indeed kill me. Would I not then be free? Not to search, of course, but free at least to rest, and to cease hoping. Yet I knew even then that he would not kill me. I was completely and solidly and livingly myself.

"Forgive me for threatening you," he said, at length. "It was only a test. You clearly believe in the truth of what you've told me. And so if you are not tricking me, then evidently it's you that has been tricked. We must seek the explanation in that area. You have described Amadea's house to me, and I shall check that description, but in the meantime we must go over the events of that day very carefully. If all that you have said is true . . ."

"It *is*!" I cried yet again.

"Very well . . . you spoke, did you not, of a light —the light that shone from the woman you took for a woman of light."

"She was covered in light."

"Now that may give us a clue. You say that she touched you, and the next thing you knew was that you were a coachman."

"Yes, sir."

"But between the touching and your becoming a coachman, you remember nothing."

"It happened so quickly . . ."

40

"Ah! Ah!" said Dr. Richter. "But did it? That's the gap in your story. How do you know that hours, days, weeks, months even, did not elapse between her touching you and your becoming a coachman—if you ever were a coachman?"

"Sir, it happened at once."

"You *thought* it happened at once. Robert, have you heard of mind-bending?"

"No, sir."

"Colleagues of mine have been experimenting recently on the influence one human mind can have over another. What in the old days the common people attributed to witchcraft we think may be due to the strength of one will subjugating another. Perhaps the woman you saw was trying the same experiment on an animal mind. After all, if the human will can be subjugated, why not the lesser will of an animal?"

"But I was a coachman, sir. She did make me into a coachman."

"I shall have to check your story with someone who was there that night. But of course, even if it were all true, you could have been there as yourself, observing all that happened, and believing all the while that you were participating as a man. This requires a lot of thought, Robert, and I have inquiries to make. But I think we're on the right lines now. Patient inquiry—the hallmark of the true scientist."

He decided to end the questioning until he had made his inquiries. It seemed that he meant to check on everything I had told him about Amadea's house and the happenings outside the Prince's Palace. I begged him to go to Amadea herself, but he said that would be difficult.

I did not see Dr. Richter for two whole days. During this time Mrs. Dumpling came in regularly to feed me and to clean my cage, but she was careful not to give me any chance of escaping. In fact, I would probably not have taken the chance even if it had been offered, because I was far too curious to learn what the scientist had discovered. In the few conversations I had with Mrs. Dumpling—punctuated at regular intervals with "Fancy that! A talking rat!"—I gathered that Dr. Richter was indeed a famous scholar who knew all there was to know about everything. Mrs. Dumpling held him in the highest esteem, and she assured me that if anyone could find out what had happened to me, Dr. Richter could. I could scarcely wait to see him again, so that when he entered my room on the third day, I was at once atremble with excitement.

VII

Dr. Richter had a good deal to report. He had been to Amadea's house and had interviewed the widow and two daughters. They and the house had been exactly as I had described, but of course he had never doubted that I had been there. He had, however, questioned them very closely about the 'woman of light', and they had been quite adamant that no such person existed. There were occasional visitors, but none corresponded to my account. On the evening of the ball, the widow had been in the house all the time, but she had heard and seen nothing out of the ordinary.

"But she would have been upstairs," I interrupted Dr. Richter. "The rest of us were downstairs—in fact the transformation took place outside in the front garden."

"Or so you believe," he said.

"Well even if you don't believe me," I said, "you'll have to admit that Amadea did go to the ball in a golden coach, and she was wearing beautiful clothes, and there were horses . . ."

"Yes indeed," said Dr. Richter. "Her going to the ball is beyond dispute, and I've checked with several of the coach drivers who were there. They all confirm that there *was* a golden coach, and there *was* a coach driver named Robert."

"There you are then," I cried. "That proves it!"

"No, no, not so fast," he said. "You really haven't got a very scientific brain, have you? Still, perhaps that's the difference between men and rats, eh? Now what does it prove? Think about it. It proves only that there was a coach and a coachman. It doesn't prove that *you* were the coachman."

"But I was."

"Think scientifically. You *believe* you were."

"I was."

"Repetition is not proof, Robert. Now I'll tell you what I think happened. Amadea must have an influential friend somewhere—unknown to the mother and the sisters. This friend provided the coach, the clothes and so forth. This much is straightforward. No magic is required there, eh? Are you with me? Now this same friend when calling for Amadea secretly that evening, saw you and conducted a remarkable experiment on you. What you took to be light was in fact an instrument designed to lull your mind, so that he—or more probably she, since you are so positive that it was a woman—could exert an influence on it. You were made to believe that you were the coachman, and you were made to believe that you could talk, and talk you can. What puzzles me, however, is that this truly remarkable person should have allowed you to go free, rather than following up the results of her experiment. That is the only mystery in the whole story."

"What about the horses that turned back into mice?" I asked. "Are you telling me that they'd been tricked as well?"

"Ah!" he exclaimed. "Now that part of the story is very interesting. The three coachmen I spoke to all confirmed that there were six white mice, and there was also a pumpkin. But . . . and this is where your story differs from theirs . . . they say the pumpkin had come from the Palace kitchens. They assume—all of them, mind—that the mice had been attracted to that spot by the pumpkin."

"But the coach and the horses . . ."

"Patience, patience! I asked them about the coach and the horses. And they maintain that the coach and the horses disappeared at the same time as the coachman, and . . . now this is the critical point . . . they all disappeared at the same time as—and I've checked this with some friends who were at the ball—at the same time as Amadea. That is to say, at midnight. There is no connection between the horses and the mice, between the coach and the pumpkin, or if it comes to that, between Robert the coachman and Robert the rat. The *only* connection that exists is inside your mind. What actually happened is that Amadea went off in her coach, while you saw those unfortunate mice being done to death by the crowd. Quite simple, really."

"It's not what happened."

"It's not what you think happened. But you see, Robert, we scientists know that different eyes perceive different things, and the world we think we see is frequently not the world that *is*. Let me show you something."

He picked up my cage, and carried me out of the room, down the stairs, through the kitchen, and out into the garden behind the house.

Dr. Richter put me down on the grass, and then walked away from me. Suddenly he was bathed in light.

"What do you see, Robert?" he asked.

"You're covered in light, sir," I said.

"Exactly!" he said. "Like the woman of light?"

"Very similar."

"But there is no mystery, Robert. I'm standing against the sun. From where you are, I would appear to be covered in light, but in fact the light is coming from behind me."

"But when I saw the woman of light, sir," I said, "it was in the evening. There wasn't any sun."

"The sun, the moon," said Dr. Richter, "a torch, perhaps—any strong light would have the same effect. What I'm trying to prove to you, Robert . . ." and here his voice took on a rather impatient edge . . . "is that things that appear to be magic can in fact have a very simple explanation. You understand?"

"Yes, sir," I replied.

There seemed little point in arguing with him, as he had clearly made up his mind that his explanation was the right one. All that interested him now was finding the scientist who had—as he put it—"bent" my mind. In this respect, we did have a common goal, for his scientist and my woman of light were one and the same person. However, his only clue as to her identity was my description of her, and this was both vague and, in his eyes, untrustworthy. He scarcely knew where to begin the search. Yet again I begged him to consult Amadea.

"It's not so easy to see princesses," said Dr. Richter. "Besides, she might not want anyone to know about this business. It's dangerous to meddle in the private lives of royalty. The equivalent for you would be to ask for a sip of the cat's milk. No, we shall have to find other means of locating this mysterious lady, if she *is* a lady."

Dr. Richter's other means proved to be rather unsuccessful. I saw less and less of him as the days went by, and it was Mrs. Dumpling who kept me informed of what was happening. He was inquiring among his colleagues, and he had put advertisements in various newspapers and magazines. But he was also very busy writing a book called "Delusions of Perception". Mrs. Dumpling didn't know exactly what this meant, but she thought Dr. Richter was proving in this book that there was no such thing as magic.

One day she brought a magazine in to show me Dr. Richter's advertisement. She read it out to me:

"Renowned scientist seeks help in training animals to talk. Handsome payment."

There were quite a lot of replies to this advertisement. Dr. Richter brought the applicants to see me, but none of them resembled the woman of light, and after a while he sent Mrs. Dumpling along instead of coming himself. She told me in secret one day that they all came hoping for the handsome payment, but she didn't think any of them knew how to make animals talk.

I began to despair. If Dr. Richter's inquiries failed and the advertisements brought nothing, what hope was there of finding my salvation? The answer, it seemed, was none. However, Mrs. Dumpling came in one morning and told me that something *was* going to happen after all. Dr. Richter had invited some of his most distinguished colleagues—"ever such clever men,' she said— to meet me. They would be coming that evening.

A little later, Dr. Richter himself came to see me.

"I'm sorry I've neglected you of late," he said, "but I've been rather busy on my book. I had hoped to use your case as an example, but it's difficult to bring you in without knowing how that confounded woman took over your mind. So I've left you out altogether. Now then, these people who are coming tonight. It's all rather unfortunate. I'd meant to keep you a secret, but word seems to have got around—I suppose because of that advertisement of mine. There are so many of my colleagues who want to meet you that I decided to invite them all together and have done with it. But they'll be asking you questions, and it's rather important that you should give them the right answers. I don't want you to come out with all this woman of light nonsense, you understand? The people you'll be meeting are scholars, and you'd make me into a bit of a laughing stock if you came out with that. So I'd like you to tell them . . . tell them you were captured in a trap, and you can only remember being confronted with a light. After that, you remember nothing until you woke up able to speak. I'd rather you didn't mention Amadea either, because some of my colleagues have important contacts, and there could be trouble if we started spreading funny rumours."

"You want me to lie," I said.

"It's not a lie!" said Dr. Richter. "The lie is the story that you told me—even though you believe it yourself. The truth is that we don't know what happened to you. And so it's best to *say* we don't know. You were trapped, you saw a light—possibly shone by a woman—and the rest is a blank."

Dr. Richter's attitude disturbed me. At first I had liked him, but now I began more and more to think of my father. "Man is to be feared at all times," he had said. This man had seemed so mild, so un-monsterlike, and yet now he was trying to force me to lie, and he was bullying my true story out of existence. I could expect no help from him, because he wanted only to use me, and as he had me in his power, I could expect no mercy from him if I disobeyed. But what was the alternative? Already he had lost interest in me. Soon I should probably be left to die in my cage. Perhaps this meeting would be my last chance of getting help from anybody. I resolved that I would disobey Dr. Richter, and take the consequences.

VIII

Dr. Richter himself carried me into the drawing-room. There must have been about twenty people sitting round the room, all men, and nearly all with bald heads and spectacles. There was a murmuring and rustling as we entered, and I noticed how all the men sat forward in their chairs, trying to get a better view of me. It was a strange feeling, knowing that every one of them could kill me and yet every one of them now wanted to hear me and talk to me, as if somehow I were more powerful than them.

"This is Robert," said Dr. Richter. "As some of you may know, I've spent a good deal of time and money trying to find whoever it was that taught Robert the power of speech. Unfortunately without success. And for Robert himself this is a mystery—there seems to be a gap in his memory which no amount of questioning can bridge. However, you're welcome to ask him questions, and of course you would all want a demonstration of his abilities. Robert, perhaps you could say a few words."

I deemed that it was not yet the right moment to bring up the subject that was of such vital importance to me. First, I must win their attention and respect.

"Gentlemen," I said, "I only hope that I shan't disappoint you. I shall endeavour to answer your questions honestly and sensibly, but of course I lack the intelligence to match yours if you should wish to debate with me. I'm ready to tell you whatever you want to know."

There were gasps all round the room, and I heard words like 'remarkable' and 'extraordinary' repeated a few times. At length a man with a bushy moustache asked:

"To what extent do you feel like a human being and to what extent like a rat?"

I could feel Dr. Richter's eyes upon me, and I knew that he was willing me not to mention the fact that I *was* human. At this stage, I would play the game his way.

"Sir," I replied, "I feel myself to be human in all respects but form. If someone were to wave a magic wand and give me a human body, I should be perfectly at ease, although clearly lacking in your education."

"Are you able to converse with other rats?" came a voice.

"No, sir. I lost that ability when I gained human speech."

"How do other rats react to you?"

"I was driven out of the nest by my own family. I'm no longer regarded as a member of that species."

"What are your feelings about that?"

It was easy for me to answer these questions, and gradually I went through my whole life story up to the moment when I had stepped into the trap. We were now approaching the critical point. I had not yet mentioned whose house I had been trapped in, but I could already feel that Dr. Richter was very tense.

"I think perhaps Robert has given sufficient demonstration of his powers," he said. "I shouldn't wish to strain him . . ."

"It's quite all right, Dr. Richter," I said. "I shall be happy to continue so long as these gentlemen want me to."

There were murmurs of approval, and Dr. Richter made a gesture of resignation. At once a very thin, long-faced man asked me to recall my last moments of rat-dom.

"Certainly, sir," I said. "But I must warn you that Dr. Richter and I have a very different interpretation of those events. Indeed he was anxious that I should not tell you my version of the story. . . ."

"Robert!" said Dr. Richter, glaring at me.

"No, no, Richter, let him go on!" said the thin man. There were noises of agreement from all round the room, and again Dr. Richter had to give way.

"Thank you, gentlemen," I said. "I shall now tell you everything that I remember, as I remember it."

And I proceeded to do just that. I spared no detail, and I even cited the confirmation provided by Dr. Richter's own inquiries. I was listened to in total silence. I brought the story right up to the present moment, and then I ended with this appeal:

"Gentlemen. In my present state I am neither one creature nor another. I live in a cage. I am fed as if by charity, and I know that if Dr. Richter wished it, I could be killed from one day to the next. My only hope is that somehow the woman of light will be found and will have the grace to transform me to what I was on that fateful evening: namely, a human being like yourselves. I am appealing to you for help."

The silence continued long after I had spoken. It was finally broken by Dr. Richter himself.

"The story you've just heard is, I must confess, exactly the story Robert told me when he first came to me. I had asked him not, under any circumstances, to mention the Princess Amadea by name. It could prove highly embarrassing to her and, of course, to ourselves. We all know that there is a widespread belief in witchcraft, and although as a scientist I totally reject such hypotheses, we do not live in an enlightened world. From a purely scientific point of view, of course, Robert's story is unbelievable. Clearly he was subjected to a process of mental influence by a remarkably advanced practitioner, and I have sought this person in vain. I totally reject Robert's charge that I tried to suppress his story. I merely wished to prevent embarrassment all round. And I must ask you to keep all that has been said strictly to yourselves. If just once it were to be rumoured that the Princess Amadea had indulged in the black arts, it could have appalling consequences. Either for her, or for those responsible for the rumour."

Dr. Richter's mention of witchcraft had made me shudder. I remembered all too vividly the terrible scene I had witnessed in the market square.

"Then I must point out," I said with as much emphasis as I could muster, "that the woman of light seemed to me to personify goodness and not evil, and what she did caused harm to no-one except to myself, and that I am sure was by pure mischance."

"You must understand, Robert," said Dr. Richter with surprising gentleness, "that we do not *believe* in fairies or witches. But outside these walls are people who *do* believe in such things, and they are dangerous."

The others all seemed to agree with him, but I could not tell whether their agreement also applied to his interpretation of my story. If they were all like him, then I had no hope of ever finding the woman of light again.

"I must apologize," I said. "I would not have mentioned the name if I had realized the danger. But my appeal to you still stands. Help me to find the woman of light, so that I can claim my true identity."

A fairly young man who had brown hair and no glasses said:

"I'm not so sure which *is* your true identity. I mean, if your own account is true, you were only human for one evening, weren't you? But you've been a rat all your life. Culturally you must still be a rat. Can you read or write?"

"No," I said.

"Plenty of humans can't read or write," said a voice.

"What do you know about art, music, literature, finance, commerce?" persisted the young man. "What do you know about government, education, history, geography? Language doesn't make a species."

"What are you trying to prove, Jenkins?" asked the thin, long-faced man.

"I'm suggesting to our friend," said Jenkins, "that if he *did* find his woman of light, he'd be better off asking her to give him back his rat language."

"It's an interesting observation," said the shiniest head in the room, "but doesn't get us very far. Unless . . . ha ha . . . Jenkins . . . ho ho . . . actually believes in women of light!"

"Could I ask you something?" I called out, when the laughter had died down. They seemed a little surprised, but the young man called Jenkins told me to ask away. "Why do you all laugh at the idea of a woman of light?"

"Let me answer that," said Dr. Richter. "We laugh, my dear Robert, because we are scientists. We know that such things do not exist."

"No we don't," interrupted Jenkins. "We *think* such things do not exist. But Robert's right to question us. Until we find a sure explanation, we have no right to laugh at his."

"You're still young, Jenkins," said the thin man. "You'll learn."

"I hope," said Jenkins, "that I'll learn not to say I know when I mean I think."

"There's no such thing as magic," said Dr. Richter sharply. "Magic is unscientific."

"That only means," said Jenkins, "that science is not equipped to study magic. The eye can't see the wind, but you don't deny that the wind exists."

There were some hostile whisperings, and I heard one bald-headed man ask another: "Who is this fellow Jenkins? What's he study?" The other replied that Jenkins was an expert on human behaviour, and had written a famous book called '*Man: King of the Beasts*'.

It seemed to me that they had all forgotten me, and I was as far as ever from a solution to my problems. I therefore called out again, asking them what was to happen to me. I had to repeat the question several times before they paid attention to me.

"Yes, what *are* you going to do with him, Richter?" someone asked.

"From my point of view," said Dr. Richter, "I've reached a dead end. I've tried to study him scientifically, but as he can tell me very little about what happened to him, and as I've failed to trace the person responsible for his condition, I think I've gone as far as I can go."

"It's a very curious case," said the thin man. "One ought to be able to make more of it really."

"He'd be very useful," said the shiny head, "if we wanted to know all about rats, eh? But who wants to know about rats, ha ha!"

"I do."

The voice came from a tiny man who sat next to Jenkins. He had not spoken before. Now everybody turned, as I did, to look at him. His hair was thin and wispy, and he wore rimless spectacles, but on examining him more closely I saw that he was quite young. His face was narrow, pinched almost, but unlined, and he had a sharp pointed nose from beneath which protruded a few stiff strands of moustache. In appearance he was remarkably like one of my own brothers. His voice was high and penetrating. I felt an instant fear of him.

"What do you want to study rats for, Devlin?" asked the man called Jenkins.

"Why does anybody study anything?" asked Devlin. "I think I may learn something from him."

"That's interesting," said Jenkins. "I was thinking of asking permission for him to learn something from me."

"You want to educate him, do you, Jenkins?" asked the thin man who had spoken earlier.

"It would be worth an effort," said Jenkins. "To see how far he could go."

"There you are, then, Richter," said the thin man. "Two offers to take him off your hands. You're the owner—you decide."

"No-one is my owner!" I cried, before Dr. Richter could say a word. "I've been trapped and I've been kept a prisoner, but that doesn't make me anybody's property!"

"Well said!" murmured Devlin.

"If I have to remain a prisoner," I said, "and if I'm to be passed on like an object with no feelings, then at least I should be consulted as to where I go."

I had expected Dr. Richter to be angry, but instead he smiled and gently patted the bars of my cage.

"Easy now, Robert," he said. "No offence intended. Gentlemen, I don't mind which of you takes Robert,

54

so long as you promise to look after him well. Mrs. Dumpling will be able to advise you how best to feed him and so on. Though no doubt Robert will also be free with his advice. Robert, which of these two gentlemen would you prefer to accompany?"

"Jenkins," I said, without hesitation.

"Then Jenkins it shall be," said Dr. Richter.

And thus it was that I changed hands yet again.

IX

Jenkins lived in two rooms at the top of a large house in the centre of town. He was obviously nothing like as rich as Dr. Richter, but his rooms were filled almost to overflowing with books. During the journey (which had been on foot) both of us had been silent, each busy with his own thoughts, but when he had shown me his room, he set me on a table and sat down beside me. His face was friendly, and I gave a little shudder of relief when I thought of Devlin and my narrow escape.

"I feel very unhappy at the idea of your being in a cage," said Jenkins. "At the same time, I've given my word to Dr. Richter that I'll look after you, and in any case you are so unique that I dare not let you escape. I should very much like to help you and be friends with you, and it would be a good start to our relationship if I could let you out. But you would have to promise me faithfully that you would not try to escape."

"Thank you," I said. "I give you that promise."

He gazed at me for a moment, and then lifted the door of my cage. I came out on to the table and looked up at him.

"I'm glad you offered to take me," I said. "I was afraid of the man called Devlin."

"Devlin's all right," said Jenkins. "He's got weird ideas, but they're only words. He's quite harmless really."

"What do you intend to do with me?" I asked.

"Well, as I said before, you're singularly lacking in education. I should like to try and teach you to read and write, and then we shall see how much human culture you can absorb. Perhaps when you've got to know more about our society, you'll be able to compare it with yours. We might even write a book together, comparing the two societies."

The idea of learning about human culture excited me. What Jenkins had said at the meeting about my general ignorance, and that I should ask the woman of light to change my language and not my form, had struck home. I knew that he was right.

"Why, though," I asked, "are you helping me when you think I should go back to my original culture?"

"Because," he said, "I don't think you *can* go back."

"You mean I shan't find the woman of light?"

"I doubt it."

"But you do believe my story, don't you?" I persisted.

"I try to keep an open mind on such matters," he said. "We don't know enough to pass judgement."

My lessons began that very evening, and they were to continue for many weeks. I will not dwell on the methods or the rate of progress, save to say that Jenkins was a model teacher and my debt to him is incalculable. I devoured every item of knowledge that he put before me, and very soon I had begun to read book after book, regardless of subject or size. Even Jenkins was amazed at the speed and the eagerness with which I learned.

"Books," I said to him one day, "are the difference between your species and mine. Everything learned, everything thought, everything experienced—you pass it all on. Nothing is ever lost. No wonder you rule the world.'

"Yes," he said, "if a man could read every book, he might indeed become knowledgeable. Though there isn't time even to read the few that I have."

"You mean there are more than these?" I cried.

"These are just a tiny number. If every book ever written were to be laid on the earth, there wouldn't be a blade of grass to be seen in the whole world."

From time to time Jenkins would play me music. He had a recorder, and with the pure delicate notes of that instrument he could fill me with any mood that pleased him. No matter how deeply immersed in my books I might be, he had only to begin playing, and I would be drawn away as surely as if I were on the end of a string.

"With your music," I said to him one day, "you could charm me over the cliff's edge."

"Music," he said, "is the purest expression of the soul. It links us to Nature, the stars, the other world. But it's for enjoyment, not for use, although its very appeal to the soul has inspired men. Music is often played in times of war."

If he had played his music all day, I should have read no books. But he wanted me to read. He would lay the books down on the table before me, and then leave me to work through them. I could turn the pages for myself, and I would break off only to eat and drink when he brought my food in. Often I would not stop even then.

One day I surprised him by asking for his own book "Man: King of the Beasts". He gave it to me, and I read it in a single afternoon. In it, he showed how man had risen above the beasts in two ways: firstly, by using technology to overcome his own natural weaknesses; secondly, by his art, which enabled him to enrich his own life through the works of others. Animals, he claimed, lived to survive, whereas man lived to survive and to enjoy. Once again Jenkins had found words that struck home very deeply. I recalled those early days when I had wanted more than the ordinary life of my species, and I recalled the evening of the ball which had opened up paradise to me.

A particular source of wonderment to me was what Jenkins called 'literature'. I read novel after novel and play after play, and felt afterwards that it was I who had lived the lives described. What the characters endured, I endured, and what they thought, I thought. Soon I knew what it was like to love, hate, rise, fall, win, lose in a thousand ways. I knew how kings and peasants lived and died, and I could take on every identity offered to me.

"It's amazing!" I cried to Jenkins. "A man could live an infinite number of lives and yet never leave his library!"

The weeks and months that I spent in Jenkins' home were the source of a lifetime's knowledge and experience. Jenkins himself was always kind to me, and we would often discuss things long into the night. He had many theories about life—its origins, its development, its purpose, and he seemed to enjoy explaining them to me and answering my questions. He seemed particularly interested in the idea that all forms of life—himself and myself included—had developed from a single common ancestor. I found it hard to believe that the ant and the elephant should have sprung from the same source, but he explained that the earth itself had undergone many violent changes, and these would certainly have brought equally violent changes to the composition of living cells. I mention this theory only because at the time it seemed to have some relevance to my own condition. I realize now, however, that no catastrophe in Nature could possibly have transformed me from rat to coachman *and then back again.* Not in a million years, let alone in the space of a few hours. I must confess, though, that I find it equally impossible to believe that even a thousand million years could transform an amoeba into an elephant, a humming bird, or a man.

Our discussions were animated, but always calm and respectful. Not so the discussions that took place between Jenkins and his friend Devlin. These were not about Art or about Nature, but about politics. Devlin had vehement views about the structure of society, and he wanted it radically changed. He believed in an even distribution of wealth and the abolition of privilege, and he would rail against the Prince, who gave lavish balls whilst there were still poor people in the town whose ribs showed through their rags. At such moments Jenkins would agree with him and I, too, could see the reasonableness of his opinions. But then he would talk with passion of mobilizing the people and overthrowing the government, and Jenkins would accuse him of demagogy and would insist that the people must be thought of as individuals and not as a mere instrument for political upheaval.

"Let them be individuals after the blood-letting," Devlin would cry. "We cannot have equality till we have rid ourselves of the causes of inequality."

"But bloodshed is not the way to end inequality," Jenkins would insist. "Your violence will only breed more violence."

They would argue for hours, and I would sit on the arm of Jenkins' chair, listening and learning.

So the months passed. It was without doubt the most fruitful period of my life, and it seems strange that I should ever have wanted it to end. But my remark that one could live infinitely without ever leaving the library proved two-edged. For all the pleasure, such living was second-hand. I began to want to live my own life, to be part of a world beyond walls and pages, where there would be things and not words describing things. I thought of the coachmen's ball, of the lips that I had kissed, of six white horses clattering over cobbles. But for all my education, I was still no nearer to becoming the human I felt myself to be. Jenkins had given me the culture, but only the woman of light could give me the shape.

I had promised Jenkins that I would not try to escape, and in any case I had no desire to lose such a friend. I openly told him my feelings, and he then asked me what I wanted to do.

"I must go and see Amadea," I said. "Only she will know where I can find the woman of light."

"It's not so easy to get appointments with princesses," said Jenkins.

"But I wouldn't need an appointment," I said. "I can just slip into the Palace, find her and talk to her. I know her, and she's kind and gentle. She'll understand."

"If you were seen going into the Palace, you'd probably be killed,' said Jenkins.

"I'll take care not to be seen," I said. "I'll wait till evening, and I'll stay in the shadows. I haven't forgotten all my training, you know."

"It's too dangerous," said Jenkins.

"There's no other way," I insisted. "It's what I want. It's the only thing I want."

At that moment, Devlin called, and Jenkins asked what he thought of the idea. To my surprise, Devlin was enthusiastic. In fact, he offered to help. He said that he knew a guard at the Palace. He would take me there himself, and get the guard to show me where to find Amadea. That way, there would be far less danger. He would even arrange for the guard to bring me out again, and would wait to carry me home.

Jenkins was pleased with the idea, and I should have been pleased too. But my fear of Devlin was stronger than ever, and I hated the idea of being in his hands even for a minute. I hesitated.

"What are you afraid of?" asked Jenkins. "I think it's a splendid plan."

I could find no reason for rejecting the offer, and finally Jenkins said that I must either go with Devlin or not go at all.

"Will you come with us?" I asked.

"I don't think my friend the guard would be so co-operative if someone else was present," said Devlin.

"It's better if there's just the two of you," said Jenkins.

Involuntarily I began to tremble. Jenkins noticed.

"You don't have to go at all, Robert," he said. "If you are frightened."

"No, I want to go," I said. "I'm just nervous."

Devlin went away, but my nervousness stayed with me throughout the day and had not left me by the time Devlin returned. My fear, let me hasten to repeat, was not of meeting Amadea but of being with Devlin. However, he picked me up with great delicacy, stroked my head with his long fingers, and then asked if I would prefer to travel in his hand or in his pocket. I chose the pocket. He wore a long coat, and gently placed me inside the deep pocket in such a way that I could poke my head out.

"Do be careful, though," said Jenkins. "And remember that Amadea is a princess now. She has a lot of power. If you think you're in danger, run."

61

"You seem to have forgotten," I remarked, "that for us rats, the first law is survival."

"So long as *you* haven't forgotten it," said Jenkins, with a little smile.

He gave my poked-out head a little pat, shook hands with Devlin, and walked with us to the door. We were going to have to make the journey on foot—or at least on Devlins's feet. Neither Devlin nor Jenkins could afford to hire a coach. I settled down in the pocket and thought about what I would say to Amadea.

X

As we walked through the streets, I noticed that Devlin was greeted by a lot of people. It surprised me that a man who had seemed so withdrawn at Dr. Richter's house should yet have so many acquaintances. Some of those who greeted him called him Mr. Devlin, and others said 'sir'. The ordinary people seemed to have great respect for him. Jenkins had told me that he and Devlin had been students together, and so I had somehow associated Devlin with books rather than with people.

It was getting dark, and the further we walked, the fewer people we met. For once, I found the absence of humans disturbing. I did not want to be alone with Devlin. But he walked briskly on, and gave not the slightest sign of wishing me harm. Indeed he stopped two or three times to inquire if I was all right.

Eventually we crossed the bridge and reached the tree-lined avenue, and now my head began to pound at the closeness of the meeting. Would I be safe in the Palace, would I be able to see Amadea at all, what would she say to me, would I see the woman of light, and would the woman of light grant my wish? One part of me wanted to cry out to Devlin to turn back. But back to what? Living and dying in books?

I could now see the flight of stone steps up to the golden door. There were no coaches, there was no music, and the door was closed. Two guards stood outside, and the splendid building that had been so warm and welcoming before now looked grey and forbidding.

Devlin did not go up the steps. Instead he walked round to the side of the Palace, where the walls merged with the shadows. Suddenly his hand was feeling my head, and I almost bit him.

"I'm going to have to leave you here for a moment," he said. "My friend will be on duty at the back gate. Wait here while I talk to him."

Gently he lifted me out of his pocket, and set me down in the darkness.

"I'll be back soon," he said.

I watched him disappear into the shadows, and then crept after him. For all his gentleness, I still didn't trust him. Fortunately, although I had lost the language of my species, I had retained the stealth. He saw and heard nothing of me. I followed him round to the back of the Palace, and there indeed was a gate, dimly lit and guarded by a single soldier.

"Evening, John!" whispered Devlin.

"Why, Mr. Devlin, sir!" exclaimed the soldier quite loud.

"Sh!" said Devlin. "I don't want anyone to know I'm here. Now listen, John, I've got a job for you."

Then he went very close to the guard and talked so low that although I crawled to within a few feet of them I could still make out nothing of their conversation.

"All right, then," said the guard at length. "Only don't let nobody in."

"You can trust me," said Devlin. "I'll go and get him."

I scurried back to the spot where Devlin had left me.

"Robert!" he whispered. "Come!"

"I'm here!" I said, and went to meet him.

"I've fixed it with the guard," he said. "He'll take you to Amadea, and he'll wait for you. But try to make your meeting brief. The guard isn't supposed to leave his post, and I shall be standing in for him. We're all running a grave risk."

"I'll be as quick as I can," I said.

He picked me up and carried me round the building to the guard.

"Talking rat, eh?" said the guard. "That'll set the tongues a-wagging."

"But not your tongue, John. Keep yours still," said Devlin rather sharply.

"Oh, I will, sir," said the guard, and took me from Devlin. Then he unlocked the door he had been guarding.

"Robert!" whispered Devlin. "One thing more. Whatever happens to-night, you're to come back to me, you understand? Your friends are counting on you."

"Of course I shall come back," I said.

"Good luck, then," he said, and the guard carried me inside the Palace, closing the door behind him.

We walked along a dark damp passage, and at once I heard the familiar sound of scampering feet. My kind will hunt anywhere. At the end of the passageway, turning to the right, was a broader way, on either side of which instead of walls were iron bars. Behind these were emaciated men in rags, and at our approach several of them came to the bars and held out their arms. "Mercy!" they cried, and "Help us!" but the guard strode on, taking no notice.

"Who are they?" I asked.

"Just prisoners," he said. "These are the dungeons."

We climbed a flight of stone steps and emerged into a lighted corridor where we were greeted by a large black cat. It saw me at once, snarled, and clawed at the guard's leg.

"Get out of it!" he snapped, and kicked the cat away. It yowled and kept its distance. I peered round the guard as we walked on, and the cat and I watched each other until we mounted another flight of stairs and were out of view.

"Lots of cats here," said the guard. "It's to keep the rats down—oh, no offence!"

"I hope Amadea won't have any with her," I whispered.

"Well, keep your claws crossed," he said.

A tall man in a black and gold uniform suddenly came round the corner towards us. John just had time to put me behind his back.

"Evening, John," said the tall man. "Aren't you supposed to be on duty?"

"Yes, sir," said John, "but I've been relieved at the back gate. There's reports of some minor disturbance at the front—nothing to worry about, only they wanted a few reinforcements, just to make sure."

"Good night then, John."

"Good night, sir."

John stood aside to let the tall man pass, and carefully kept me out of sight.

"That was the major domo," whispered John. "We were lucky. He normally pokes his nose into everything.

Probably in a hurry for his tipple. Likes the bottle does the major domo. He drinks more in a night than I earn in a week."

We came to a door, and John stopped.

"Now, this is the trickiest bit," he said. "Will she be here or won't she? And will she be on her own?"

He looked round, then bent down to place me on the red-carpeted floor. Slowly he pressed the door-handle and eased the door slightly open. I poked my head through the crack.

In a beautiful chair of velvet and gold sat Amadea, engrossed in a large book of fairy-tales. There was no-one else in the room. I looked up at John.

"It's all right," I whispered. "She's alone."

I squeezed into the room, and John gently closed the door behind me.

XI

"Excuse me," I said.

Amadea jumped in her chair, and a startled look came into her blue eyes. The look turned to one of puzzlement as she searched for the owner of the voice.

"I'm down here," I said. "At the side of your chair."

She looked down and saw me.

"Oh!" she said. "You startled me."

"I'm sorry," I said. "Only I have to talk to you."

"I've never seen a rat that talked before," she said. "It's almost as if you'd stepped out of this book I'm reading."

"You don't remember me, do you?"

She looked puzzled again. "Should I remember you?"

"I'm Robert, your coachman."

Her mouth opened in surprise. Then she leaned down and held out her hand to lift me up. I was far too big, and her finger nails hurt my stomach as she hoisted me up. She put me on her lap and once more I was able to look into those sky-blue eyes. There was a clearness and freshness about her that made me want to melt.

"On the last stroke of midnight, you changed back into a rat," she said. "Poor Robert. Where have you been since then? What's been happening to you?"

Very briefly I told her everything that had passed: my being driven out of the nest, my capture by Mister Biggs, his selling me to Dr. Richter, and my transference to the kind-hearted Jenkins.

"But now," I said, "I've come to you because I must have your help. I can't go on as I am. In all things except my body I'm human."

"How can *I* help you?" she asked.

"By telling me where to find the woman of light. She's the only one with the power to change me back."

"Of course!" she said. "It was she who changed you in the first place! But to find her . . . I never went to her, you see. She always came to me. When I'm in trouble she comes, but I don't know how to summon her."

"If I can't find her," I said, "I shall be for ever trapped in this body. What she did to me was very cruel."

"It's true," said Amadea, her blue eyes clouding. "We never thought of you. Please forgive us."

"Do you know that the white mice were killed?"

"Oh no!"

"I saw them beaten to death."

"But that's terrible! And it's all my fault! I was supposed to leave before midnight, but I was so happy I never noticed the time. And now all this suffering . . ."

The tears began to fall from her eyes.

"No," I said, "I'd have been turned back into a rat anyway. The mice would have been saved, but my situation wouldn't have been altered. Don't cry. It isn't your fault."

"All of you were changed to help me," she said. "It's as if I bought my happiness with your lives. But I never thought of it. I thought only of myself!"

"You couldn't know what would happen," I said. "You mustn't reproach yourself. But I do beg of you to try and help me now."

"If only I could bring her! If only I knew where she lived!"

She gazed into space as her mind desperately sought a means of contacting the woman of light. Almost absently she stroked my head as she thought, and the touch of her fingers transfixed me with pleasure. I was warmed, soothed, lulled, enhanced, and as had happened once before in my life, I wanted to preserve the moment for ever.

"Perhaps," she said, "if we were to pray for her to come . . . let's try together. Close your eyes with me and concentrate hard."

I did as she told me.

"Please come, dear Mara," she prayed earnestly. "We need you. Come now to help Robert. Please, Mara, come, we beg you!"

But the prayer was not answered.

"I don't know why it is," said Amadea. "She only comes at her will, not at mine. Oh what can we do, Robert?"

"I shall have to remain as I am," I said. "No-one else can change me. But when she does come, perhaps you'll think of me and ask her to help me."

"Oh but you must stay here until she comes," said Amadea. "I'll give you a room of your own, and servants to look after you. Then when she comes, you'll be here waiting for her and she can change you right away. And I'll make you my own coachman for as long as you like."

"It's kind of you," I said, "but I can't stay. I gave my word to my friends that I would return. Besides, there are too many cats in your palace. I'd never sleep at night."

"I'll make sure they're kept away from you. You can have guards . . ."

"No, Princess, I must go. But I'll tell you where I live, in case the woman of light does come."

I explained to her where Jenkins' house was, and she wrote the details down in the back of her book. Then she held and stroked me again. I did not want to leave, but the guard and Devlin were waiting, and they were risking their lives for me.

"I *must* go, Princess," I said.

"I'll take you then," she said. "It's not safe for you to go on your own."

"My friends are waiting. I'll be all right. Just open your door so that I can go out, but don't come into the corridor."

She did as I had asked.

"Goodbye, Robert," she said. "I'll come to you as soon as I can. I know she'll help you."

"Thank you, dear Princess," I said. "Now please close the door after me. My friend would be afraid if you were to see him."

She closed the door. I felt unutterably sad.

XII

"**Y**ou took your time," said John. "Come on, let's get moving."

He picked me up, and we retraced our steps down corridors and stairs.

"Any luck?" he asked as we walked.

"She's promised to try to help me," I said.

"Good. Mr. Devlin'll be pleased about that."

I kept my wary eye open for cats, but they stayed away from us on our return journey. Perhaps John's boots had a reputation. As we walked past the dungeons, the same begging hands reached out towards us, and the same begging voices pleaded for help and mercy. It seemed scarcely credible that upstairs there should be such gentleness and light, while in the very same house there should dwell the dark despair that I was witnessing now.

"Why are they here?" I asked John.

"Criminals," he replied. "Thieves, beggars, debtors, traitors, that's what all of them are. Don't you take no notice of them."

"Mercy!" they cried. "Help us!"

Fleetingly I wondered if the woman of light heard their voices. But then we had left the dungeons behind, and were stepping out through the rear gate and into the night.

"Mr. Devlin, sir!" called John softly.

"Here, John. Everything all right?"

Devlin came up to us.

"No trouble, sir," said John. "He's had his talk."

"Any luck?"

"He says she's promised to help him."

"Good, good. You can tell me all about it, Robert, on the way. John, you've done well tonight. I shan't forget this, you can count on me."

"Then I shall see you tomorrow, sir."

"Indeed. Come, Robert."

There were whispered goodbyes, as John handed me over to Devlin, and then we set off round the Palace wall, past the flight of steps, and on to the tree-lined avenue.

"I want to know everything that happened," said

Devlin. "Every word that passed between you. Do you think you could ride on my shoulder? There's nobody about at this time of night, so it's quite safe."

I agreed, and he put me on his shoulder so that we could talk as we walked. I told him everything, and repeated word for word the conversation I had had with Amadea. His interest surprised me, as did his enthusiastic response when I spoke of her prayer, her eagerness to help, her sorrow at the death of the white mice, and her invitation to me to stay. To all of these he responded with a warmth and pleasure that made me feel I had wronged him badly.

"She never put the blame elsewhere, then?" he commented.

The question puzzled me a little. "Of course not," I said.

"What I mean," said Devlin, "is that she has confirmed your version of all the events. The Richter explanation, for instance, is totally discredited. She attributes your change to magic and not to science."

"Oh yes," I said. "My story was the truth."

"Wonderful!" he cried. "And she even promised to bring the woman of light to you as soon as she can."

"Yes, she did."

"You're a model to us all, Robert. Truth will have its reward. How good is your memory, Robert?"

"Very good, as far as I know."

"Would you, for instance, be able to repeat this account you've given me tonight? Word for word, mind?"

"Yes, of course I would."

"Splendid! Splendid!"

"But why . . ."

"Jenkins will be delighted, as I am. But I've a favour to ask of you. I'm sure you will admit that I've helped you tonight."

"Yes, you have, and I am truly grateful. Without you, I'd never have been able to see the Princess."

"In this world, one friend must help another. You agree?"

"I do."

"Now here is my problem. Jenkins' house is much further away than mine. I have no money to hire a coach, even if one could at such a late hour. If I had to walk to Jenkins' house, and thence back to my own, I should reach home when the sun was already rising. And tomorrow I have a great deal of work to do."

"I understand!" I cried, relieved that his request should be such a minor one. "You want me to spend the night at your house."

"Precisely," he said. "Jenkins will be worried, it's true, but after all, it's scarcely my fault that we are so late. He'll understand when we explain it to him. And tomorrow there's to be an important meeting which he'll be attending as well. We shall see him then, and I can hand you over to him."

"Of course," I said. "I scarcely know how to thank you for your kindness, and your hospitality now will put me even further in your debt."

"Then that's settled," he said. "And we shall drink a glass of wine together to celebrate your success at the Palace."

We walked on. He offered to put me in his pocket, but I preferred to sit on his shoulder as I could see more. I now began to pay greater attention to the places we walked through, and I found to my surprise that they seemed vaguely familiar. I murmured something to this effect, and Devlin gave a sort of half laugh.

"It should be familiar," he said, "since you've been here often enough in thought and deed. Be patient, and I'll show you a house you know very well."

We turned a corner, and stopped outside an iron gate flanked by iron railings.

"It's Amadea's house!" I cried. "But surely you don't live here!"

"Oh no," he said. "I live in the house next door."

"Then you knew Amadea before!" I said.

"I knew her well. Or thought I did. I once asked her to marry me, but she turned me down. Perhaps even then she had dreams of marrying her prince."

There was a strange tone in his voice that disturbed me. All at once I was afraid of him again, but he swiftly altered the tone as if he had sensed my apprehension:

"The two sisters would have said yes. Only they couldn't get anyone to ask the question!" He gave a dry humourless laugh.

We walked on to the house next door, and descended a small flight of steps down to the basement, where Devlin lived. His rooms were large and bare, with just a few books but hundreds of papers piled untidily in the corners and on the chairs.

"I am not the neatest of men," he said. "But what I lack in neatness I make up for in thoroughness. Let's have our glass of wine."

He brought out two glasses, but I asked to have mine in a saucer.

"Forgive me," he said. "I'm not used to such company."

In the light I was now able to see his face properly. It was as pinched and hungry as ever, but there was an unmistakable excitement written over his features, and he seemed unable to stay still. It must have been very late by now, and yet he showed no signs of tiredness. One would have thought he was the one who had seen the Princess and been given hope for the future.

"I think we've got to know each other better tonight," he said suddenly. "I know you've never liked me, and yet I never did you any wrong."

I felt ashamed and embarrassed at these words, but I could not deny so absolute a truth.

"Perhaps it's *because* I didn't know you," I said. "I feel now that I can trust you, and as I said before, I am for ever in your debt."

"Good," he said. "It's better to be friends than enemies. I shall go on helping you to the greatest of my ability."

"Perhaps one day I shall be able to return your kindness," I said.

The wine was clearly having its effect on both of us, for these protestations of friendship and gratitude were certainly more effusive than was natural.

"You may be able to help me sooner than you think," he said. "Because now that I reflect upon the matter, I realize that you could be of enormous assistance to me as early as tomorrow."

"How?" I asked.

"This meeting I mentioned to you. It's one which, like your meeting with Amadea, will affect the whole course of my life. Many people will be there, and it's important that I should convince them of certain facts. Your help might clinch the argument in my favour."

"Tell me how I can help, and I will!" I said.

"All you would have to do is repeat what you've told me tonight. Tell them word for word what was spoken between you and Amadea."

"I'll do that with pleasure," I said, "if it really will help you."

"You must tell them the truth, though," he insisted. "The story must be yours, not Richter's."

"Richter's explanation was false. Of course I shall tell the truth."

"Then I can count on you?"

"I shall be glad to do you that service."

"Splendid! Then let's have one final drink before we shut up for the night."

He poured out more wine, and raised his glass.

"To friendship!" he said. "And truth!"

"To friendship and truth!" I said. "Forgive me if I don't raise my saucer."

He found a cushion for me to sleep on, and I lay down with a warm glow of contentment inside me. I had seen Amadea again, she had given me hope for my future, and on top of this I had made a new friend. Little did I dream that the following day would be the most terrible of my life.

XIII

It was very early the next morning when Devlin woke me. The grey light that came down through the basement window showed that the sun had scarcely begun to rise.

"Today is the day," said Devlin. "We must go now."

He put me in his pocket so that I would be out of sight, and then we set off. The streets were still almost deserted, though one or two people were up, and greeted Devlin respectfully. One of them wished him luck and said: "We're all on your side, sir." Yet again I was surprised at the extent of his acquaintanceships.

After a while we began to meet up with more and more people who were heading in the same direction as ourselves. They also knew Devlin and greeted him with expressions of support.

We came at last to the market-place where I had often performed for Mister Biggs. Peeping out from Devlin's pocket, I could see that already the square was full of people, but the stalls were not yet up, and there was an excitement abroad that was unlike the ordinary bustle I had known before. Devlin did not stop, but made his way through the crowd to a large building with a grand entrance and a clock.

"This way, Mr. Devlin," said a fat man in the doorway, "they're all waiting for you."

He took us up a flight of stairs and into a large hall which was packed with people. As soon as we entered there was a hum of interest, and all heads were turned in our direction. We went up on a raised platform at the very end of the hall. On it was a table, at which were seated five or six very serious looking men. I had not seen any of them before. Devlin took me out of his pocket and placed me on the table.

"This is your rat, is it, Devlin?" asked the nearest of the men, and peered at me over his spectacles.

I found his attention embarrassing, but held my tongue as I did not want to say anything that might harm Devlin's chances of success. Instead, I gazed round the hall, searching particularly for Jenkins. There was no sign of him, though, and to my surprise there was also no sign of Dr. Richter or the other scientists I had met.

The crowd had gradually fallen silent, and now at the centre of the table a man stood up to address them. He wore a long black gown.

"Ladies and gentlemen," he said, "we all know why we

are here. I call upon Mr. Devlin to present the evidence which he promised us."

The black-gowned man sat down, and the heads turned to watch Devlin. As he spoke, I studied the people. There were all sorts there, young and old, men and women, clean and dirty. There were none, though, that I would have thought scholars. These were ordinary folk, such as one would expect to see in the market but not at a learned meeting.

"You can all see," Devlin was saying, "that on this table there stands a rat. To outward appearances like any other. But as you will soon see, he is not like any other. Because this rat can talk."

There were murmurs and mumblings all round the hall. A woman in the front row turned to her neighbour and said: "I seen that rat afore. 'S true, him can talk! I seen him in the fairground!"

"I shall very soon ask him to talk to you," continued Devlin, "but first I should like very briefly to tell you how he acquired his power of speech. What I am about to tell you is the exact truth, and Robert himself will correct me if anything I say is inaccurate—won't you, Robert?"

"Certainly," I said.

There was another buzz all round the hall. Clearly the fame of Mister Biggs and myself had not reached all the ears that were present.

"Robert," said Devlin, "was caught in a trap in Amadea's house. This was before she became a princess, of course. She was then a simple scullery maid in servant's rags. On the night of the Prince's ball, she helped to prepare her two sisters, and when they had left she was visited by a being whom Robert has called the woman of light."

The words brought a few titters from the audience, but Devlin quickly silenced them.

"If the term seems funny to you, then wait till you hear the rest of this story. Robert saw Amadea take out a pumpkin and six white mice. Then he himself was carried to the woman. Robert, perhaps you will tell our friends what you saw."

"Yes," I said. "The mice had been turned into white horses, and the pumpkin into a golden coach."

More reactions from the crowd, this time louder, more strident.

"And what happened to you, Robert?"

"She touched me, and I was transformed into a coachman."

"This is how Robert learned to speak," said Devlin. "And there are witnesses here who will confirm that there *was* a golden coach, there *were* six white horses, and there *was* a coachman named Robert to whom they spoke. Jack Rowley, Tom Loxton, will you confirm that?"

Two men in the audience waved their arms and shouted that every word was true. I at once recognised them as the huge red-faced coachman I had spoken to first, and the jolly man who had given me a drink.

"Now Robert," Devlin continued, "would you say the transformation was merely an illusion, was it a scientific experiment, or was it simply magic?"

"There's no doubt at all," I said, "that it was magic."

Reactions in the crowd. Clearly they were convinced already.

"At midnight," said Devlin, "the spell ended. Amadea ran from the ball because she knew the magic was going to fade. The coach turned back into a pumpkin, the horses into mice, which were killed by the coachmen. You confirm that, Jack, Tom?"

They did.

"And Robert himself was changed back into a rat. You confirm that, Robert?"

"It's true," I said.

"Last night," he went on, "I myself took Robert to the Palace. He spoke to Amadea. She confirmed everything that had happened, and admitted that Robert's transformation was her fault. That is so, isn't it Robert?"

I agreed that it was. I should have liked to add that I did not myself blame her for anything, but Devlin continued before I could say any more.

"She most generously offered to provide Robert with a room, with servants, even with guards to protect him against the cats."

He turned to me again, and I said that it was all true.

"Most important of all, however, she promised to contact the woman of light so that Robert would be changed back into a coachman. Robert, once more I must ask you to confirm the truth of what I have said."

In fact it was not quite true. Amadea had promised to *try* and contact her woman of light. But there seemed little point in correcting such a small slip, and so I endorsed Devlin's version. Only then did it become apparent how cleverly I had been tricked.

"Now you have it!" cried Devlin. "Amadea calls upon her familiar to change pumpkins into coaches, mice into horses, rats into men! In a single evening she causes the Prince to fall so in love with her that a fortune is spent trying to find her again. And now she promises that this talking rat will be transformed again into a coachman! Can you doubt, can any of you doubt, that the woman we call Princess Amadea is in fact a witch?"

There were roars from the crowd.

"Here we have the living proof of her evil arts!" shouted Devlin. "Could a talking rat be a product of anything but witchcraft?"

Again the crowd roared.

"No, no," I cried. "Amadea's not a witch! You don't understand . . ." But my voice was drowned by the baying in the hall.

"What kind of rulers are they," shouted Devlin, compelling them to listen once again, "who would spend a fortune on dancing and feasting while their subjects are slaving, begging, starving? What kind of a princess will offer shelter, food, servants to a rat, while children suffer in the streets? How long are we to be ruled by the Prince and his witch? How long are we to endure their tyranny? How long are we to remain poor while they gorge themselves on luxury? How long? How long?"

His last words were lost in the commotion. The crowd seethed and howled, and arms waved aloft to a cry of "Kill them! Kill them!"

"Go!" cried Devlin. "Bring them to justice!"

The crowd took up the cry of "Justice!" and poured out through the doors of the hall. From outside the cries were taken up by the people in the square: "To the palace! Kill them! Justice! Burn the witch!"

Devlin turned to the men at the table.

"Nothing can stop it now," he said. "Only blood can quench that thirst."

He went to a door that opened out onto a balcony overlooking the square. The others joined him, to watch the crowd rushing off to the Palace. They had all forgotten about me, and I crouched on the table, trembling in every limb. What had I done? How had it happened? I was paralysed with horror.

I saw Devlin turn to one of his companions and laugh that strange dry laugh of his, and somehow the sound jolted me back into control of myself. Unwittingly I had helped to release these forces of destruction, and they were directed against the person I loved best in the whole world. I must warn her. Somehow I must get to the Palace before that murderous army. I leapt off the table, and raced down the stairs and out into the square.

XIV

If I had tried to run through the streets, I should certainly have been trampled to death in no time at all. My only hope was to take a route through houses and gardens. This I did, but the chances of my not being spotted by a human or chased by a cat or dog were impossibly slim. It was not long before I came face to face with a fierce snarling dog, and I only escaped by slipping through a hole in the hedge that was too small for the dog. The sight of a distant cat caused another hold-up, as I hid in a bush until it had disappeared. It was obvious that my mission was hopeless, and had been so from the start. I could never get to the Palace before that racing mob, and even if I had been able to do so, how would I have gained entry, how would I have found Amadea, and how would she have been able to escape? All I had succeeded in doing now was to put my own life in danger.

Nevertheless, I continued to make my way towards the Palace. I kept to the bushes and hedges wherever I could, and at the least sign of danger I hid and stayed still. Survival first. Eventually I came to the river bank. There seemed to be no way for me to cross. The bridge was already full of people, and to swim was impossible, for the water flowed at the speed of a galloping horse. But here luck was on my side. A cheer went up from the crowd as a coach came slowly towards the bridge. In it were Devlin and his friends. The bridge was narrow, and they had to stop while the crowd made way for them, and so I seized my chance. I ran through the grass and the rushes that separated the road from the river, and scrambled unseen onto one of the struts that held the coach together. Thus Devlin and his friends carried me across the bridge and into the tree-lined avenue. It was easy for me then to leap to the ground and scurry into the gardens that backed on to the avenue. From behind a shrub I watched the crowd jostling towards the Palace. The tramp of the feet and the human snarling and roaring were terrifying sounds. I had read of such things in Jenkins' books, and the writers always compared the mob to wild animals, but animals in my experience are incapable of such hatred and blood lust.

They swept on to the Palace. I darted from one shrub to another until I was able to take up a position from which I could see the steps and the golden gate. Two soldiers stood at the foot of the steps, and they simply disappeared beneath the waves of people. I heard cries of "Break down the door!" but this proved unnecessary, for the gate was opened from inside. No doubt John had organized that for his friend Devlin. People poured through into the Palace, and I found myself praying to the woman of light to help her. Nothing short of magic could save her from those hundreds and thousands of haters.

I could still see Devlin and his friends. They had kept at a distance from the raging mob, and Devlin made gestures to two of his men, who at once went off in different directions. Suddenly I caught sight of Jenkins. He was heading straight towards Devlin. I wanted to run out and greet him, but restrained myself because it would have been too dangerous. Devlin turned when Jenkins came near, and although I could not hear what they were saying, it was evident that they both became very angry. Several times Devlin waved Jenkins away, but Jenkins would not leave, and in the end Devlin turned to one of his men, who struck Jenkins a terrible blow on the head. He fell to the ground, and the man kicked him two or three times. I felt that it was I who had been struck and kicked.

As Jenkins lay there motionless, the two men Devlin had sent away returned. They were followed by two lines of servants who were carrying bundles of wood, and behind these were soldiers who took up positions near the steps. Devlin indicated a spot about halfway between the steps and the place where I was hiding, and the servants proceeded to lay down their wood in a pile that looked hideously familiar to me.

During this activity, Jenkins stirred, and rose unsteadily to his feet. Devlin and the others had not seen him rise, and he staggered away from them, blood streaming from his face. I broke cover and ran towards him.

"Jenkins! Jenkins!" I called. "Over here!"

He saw me, and came towards me.

"Quickly!" I said. "Into this garden!"

I raced back to the safety of my shrubs, and he joined me there. His face looked very pale beneath the blood.

"Are you all right?" I asked.

"Yes," he said. "The blood will soon dry. What happened to you?"

As briefly as I could, I told him of my meeting with Amadea and of how Devlin had tricked me.

"He's mad!" said Jenkins. "And the people are mad to follow him. Only who would have thought it? He must have been planning this for months, and I never suspected."

"What does he hope to achieve?" I asked.

"Power," he said. "Devlin's going to seize power!"

At this moment there was a loud roar from the crowd, and out of the golden gate came groups of soldiers and citizens triumphantly displaying their prisoners. I could see the Prince, Amadea, the major domo and some others, each one rudely thrust forward to the top of the steps for the crowd to jeer at. Their hands were tied behind their backs, and I saw that Amadea's hair was loose round her shoulders and her dress was torn.

Now Devlin mounted the steps. He stood directly in front of Amadea, and spat in her face. Then he turned to the crowd, raised his arms high, and cried:

"What do we do with tyrants?"

"Chop off their heads, chop off their heads, chop off their heads!" chanted the crowd.

"And what do we do with witches?" he cried.

"Burn them, burn them, burn them!" chanted the crowd.

"And what do we do with traitors?" cried the Prince.

His words were so bold, and so timely, that the whole crowd was taken aback, and could respond only with silence.

"I am no tyrant!" the Prince said. "Nor is my wife a witch! Have I oppressed you? Have I tortured you? Have I murdered you? What harm has my wife ever done? What magic has she ever used? Who accuses us of these things?"

"I do!" said Devlin. "I and the people! Your tyranny is not of oppression but of apathy. Look at these people, poorly dressed, poorly housed, poorly fed, while you live in a vast palace, adorn yourselves with gold, and fill your stomachs with more food than you can digest! You enjoy

85

the wealth while the people must do the labour! That is your tyranny, Prince!"

"Princes have lived in this palace since time immemorial," said the Prince. "The ruler rules and the governed labour. How else can the world be? If you kill us, who will rule you?"

"We shall rule ourselves!" cried Devlin. "And wealth will belong to the people, not to the Prince!"

He turned to the crowd.

"The Palace will be yours!" he cried. "And the wealth will be yours, the food, the gold, the wine! Everything will be yours! Do you want it?"

The crowd, which had listened in silence till now, greeted his offer with loud shouts of "Yes!"

"We will govern ourselves, Prince," said Devlin. "We don't need you. And we don't need your witch-wife either."

"She is no witch!" said the Prince. "You have no grounds for calling her that!"

"Yes, we have grounds," said Devlin. "Ask her who created a talking rat? Who turned mice into horses? Who makes pumpkins into gold coaches? Who has promised to make a rat into a man?"

Jenkins turned to me. "Robert," he said urgently, "will you come with me to help them?"

"Yes," I said. "We must hurry!"

Jenkins picked me up, and ran towards the steps.

"That was not witchcraft!" Amadea was saying, tears falling over her pale cheeks. "I've done no evil!"

"Rats into men, men into rats!" said Devlin. "Can this be done by anything other than black magic?"

"Yes!" cried Jenkins, and as heads turned, he forced his way through the crowd and onto the steps. "She is not a witch! This is the talking rat! He'll tell you so himself!"

He held me high above his head.

"The Princess Amadea is all goodness!" I cried. "You must not kill her! She does no magic herself! The magic —good magic—is done by the woman of light!"

"The rat talks!" shouted Devlin. "You hear the talking rat! There is your proof! Seize them!"

At once Jenkins was seized by soldiers, and at a sign from Devlin, a line of guards positioned themselves across the foot of the steps. I was still in Jenkins' hands as the soldiers held him by his neck and his clothes and dragged him up the steps to join the other prisoners. I noticed that John was one of the guards holding the Prince.

"We have been governed," cried Devlin to the crowd, "by those in league with the forces of darkness! They have prospered while we have suffered! Now is the time for us to free ourselves! The rich and evil will be punished, and their riches given to the poor! I demand justice for the people! What is to be done with the Prince? You are the people, you will govern, you will decide!"

"Chop off his head, chop off his head, chop off his head!" came the chant.

Devlin turned to John.

"Then chop off his head," he said.

"No!" cried Amadea.

"Don't cry," said the Prince. "We shan't be parted for long."

While the guards held him, John unbuttoned his tunic and tore it off him.

"And which of you is prepared to shed royal blood?" asked the Prince.

"Royal blood is no different from other men's blood," said Devlin.

"Princes are born to rule," said the Prince. "A blow against me is a blow against the natural law of this world. Who is prepared to strike against Nature?"

The soldiers looked uncomfortable, and none stepped forward.

"I'll give his clothes and his crown to the man that chops off his head," said Devlin.

At once a black-bearded guard came forward. "I'll do it," he said. "It's what the people want. It's the people's decision."

The crowd fell silent as the Prince was made to kneel on the steps, with his head resting on the top platform where we all stood. The black-bearded soldier had drawn his heavy sword, and stood beside the Prince. He raised his sword high in the air.

"I love you, Amadea," said the Prince.

Down came the sword.

XV

I cannot describe the horror of that moment. There was blood everywhere. Amadea fainted. Would that she had died in her faint. The rest of us stared at the kneeling body and the half-severed head, and once Amadea had been lowered to the ground, I think no one moved for minutes on end. The black-bearded soldier, who had received the full force of the spurting blood, stood like a crimson statue, his sword still pointing downwards, held in both hands. It was he who finally unfroze the tableau by dropping his sword, which fell with a clatter down the stone steps.

"The tyrant is dead!" shouted Devlin. "Long live the people!"

He gestured to his friends to take up the cry, and they too shouted: "The tyrant is dead!" The words were quickly gathered up by the crowd, and soon they were cheering and waving. I remembered the wedding procession. They had cheered and waved then, too.

The black-robed man who had spoken in the hall now approached Devlin.

"The witch must be burned," he said. "But we must try to make her confess and repent first."

"If she does," said Devlin, "it'll serve us well. If she doesn't, she'll still burn."

A kind-hearted woman had ministered to Amadea and given her water to drink. Now she stirred, and the black-gowned man knelt beside her.

"My child," he said, "you must confess your sins. Ask to be forgiven."

Amadea raised her head and looked at the black-gowned man in bewilderment.

"Forgiven for what?" she said. "What have I done?"

The excitement of the crowd had died down again, and Devlin now turned to them once more.

"The tyrant is dead!" he shouted. "But the witch lives! What do you want done with her? What is your decision?"

"Burn her!" came the cry from Devlin's friends.

"Burn her, burn her, burn her!" came the responding chant from the crowd.

The black-gowned man was still talking to Amadea, but I could no longer hear their words against the unceasing chant of the crowd. I could only see the tears that fell from blue eyes that were wide with terror.

The soldiers carried Amadea down the steps and through the crowd to the pile of wood. A pole had been wedged fast in the wood, and to this the soldiers now tied the Princess. She could not stand, and had to be held up until the bonds were in place. The black-gowned man had accompanied her all the way, and now stood beside the pyre, his lips moving all the time.

"How can this happen?" murmured Jenkins. "How can this be allowed to happen?"

"Burn her!" chanted the crowd.

Lighted torches were thrust under the wood. At first there were no flames, and just for a moment I thought there might be a miracle and the pyre would refuse to burn. But then the smoke rose, followed by the flames, and even from the top of the steps I could hear the first crackles.

Devlin turned to one of his companions.

"Anyway," he said, "it's appropriate that Amadea should end in ashes."

As the flames rose higher, she strained to get away from them, and when the first one bit into her flesh she cried out pitifully.

"Save her!" I prayed. "Save her, please!"

And then the miracle did happen. As the flames leapt and swayed and struck, suddenly in their midst a woman appeared. She was encased in a soft white light, and even from where I stood her beauty was overwhelming. She touched Amadea's head and the jerking body was suddenly still. Then . . . how is this to be explained? It was as if Amadea stepped forth from Amadea. The woman of light held her by the hand, and together they came out of the flames and seemed to hover above them looking down at the Amadea who had been left behind.

"Look there!" I cried to Jenkins. "Look, the woman of light!"

"Where?" he said.

"There, beside the flames!"

"I see no woman of light," said Jenkins.

And the crowd still cheered and chanted. They, too, had seen nothing.

"She was inside the flames," I said, "and she took the living Amadea out of the dead Amadea. Now they're moving away. Look! Can't you see them, moving over the crowd towards the avenue? And now the Prince is with them! I can see the Prince, too!"

"Go to them!" said Jenkins suddenly. "Save yourself while you can!"

Until that moment I had not even realized that only Jenkins' hands were holding me. He spread them wide, and I sprang to the ground and raced away down the steps. All eyes were still on the burning pyre, and no one noticed me scurry through the forest of legs and across into the avenue.

"Amadea!" I called. "Amadea! Amadea!"

And there she was, hand-in-hand with the woman of light and with the Prince.

"Stop! Oh stop!" I cried.

They did stop. I came into their presence and was bathed in that unearthly light. I was again filled with warmth and peace, and a longing to merge into them, to be one with them.

"It's Robert!" said Amadea. "My poor brave Robert."

"Take me with you!" I said to her. "Let me serve you!"

"No, that cannot be," said the woman of light in a voice that seemed to caress the air. "It's not time for you to come."

"Dearest Mara," said Amadea, "this is Robert, whom you made into my coachman. He's suffered so much. Can you not change him back into the man he longs to be?"

"Is that what you want, Robert?" asked the woman of light.

91

"Yes," I whispered, almost too overcome to speak.

"Then let it be so," she said.

She leaned down to me, and touched my head. I felt myself rise and swell. My skin seemed to split, and out of it I emerged greater and greater until I was a man.

"Now you're a coachman," said the woman of light.

I looked down at my fine uniform with gold buttons. There were shiny boots on my feet, and in my hand was a whip. I was tall.

"Mara," whispered Amadea. "A coachman must have a coach."

"And a coach he shall have," said the woman of light. "Bring me an acorn and two ants, Robert, for your coach must be a town-carriage this time."

I vaulted into the garden where I had hidden before. There were acorns a-plenty on the grass, and ants scurried all round. I picked up an acorn, and trapped two ants in the cup of my hand, then I took them back to the woman of light.

"Set them on the ground," she said.

She touched them with her wand, and they rose and swelled into a carriage drawn by two black horses.

"Now you have your heart's desire," she said. "And we must leave you."

"Goodbye, brave Robert," said Amadea. "Live well."

I wanted to say so many things to them, but no words could find their way into my mouth. I could only watch them glide away from me, further and further, until they seemed like a single cloud of light that grew ever smaller, dwindling to a glow, a star, and then nothing.

I stood there I know not how long. Then I turned, laid my face against the neck of one of my black horses, and wept.

XVI

"To the dungeons!" they were shouting. "To the dungeons, to the dungeons!"

In the distance, at the top of the steps, the guards led away the pinioned major domo, the other servants of the Prince, and my friend Jenkins, who had given me my life. What did the crowd know of Jenkins? What did the crowd know of Devlin? "To the dungeons!" they howled, and they cheered at the granting of their wish.

I climbed onto my coach and edged my horses forward to the fringe of the crowd. People began to give way.

"And now," cried Devlin, "let's enter the People's Palace!"

He and his friends passed through the golden gate, and in a great surge the crowd swept up the steps, narrowing to a head at the entrance. Soon they would all be swarming through the halls, the corridors, the chambers, the gardens, treading and trampling, smashing and crushing. Slowly I continued to push forward until I reached the foot of the steps. Then I waited while the wave of people seethed round and past me.

At the top of the steps, I could see the Prince. He was still kneeling, but now he was naked. The black-bearded executioner had claimed his payment. For all its stillness and nakedness, the body commanded respect, because

93

the wave veered away from it as if it were as rock-like as my coach. But I had no time to venerate the Prince. As soon as I saw a gap in the crowd, I jumped from my coach and ran to the side of the Palace. Along the wall where I had hidden in the shadows, and round to the door I ran. It was open. But I could not yet enter, for as I arrived there emerged a line of pitiful creatures. They were ragged and bearded and pale as the walls of the Palace. These were the prisoners I had seen the night before.

They blinked and shook their heads as they came out into the daylight. One of them spoke in a voice that shocked me by its familiarity.

"Never thought I'd live to see the day when air tasted better 'n wine!" he said. It was Mister Biggs.

I was tempted to tell him who I was, but I had not come here to see Mister Biggs. I merely asked him why he had been imprisoned.

"Thieving!" he said. "And what's it to do with you, coachman?"

I didn't wait to answer, for the last of the prisoners had come out, and the doorway was clear.

I hurried along the dark damp passageway, and turned at the end. The guards were just locking the iron grilles.

"Wait!" I called out. "There's an urgent order from Mr. Devlin. Which is the man called Jenkins?"

"I'm Jenkins," came his voice through the darkness.

"Jenkins is to be released," I said.

"Who gave the order?" asked one of the guards.

"Mr. Devlin himself," I said. "Release him at once."

I spoke with absolute authority. The keys clinked and the iron grille clanked.

"Go on, then," said the guard, "if that's what he wants."

Jenkins came towards me.

"You're to go home at once," I told him. He was now very close to me, and even in that gloom I could see the questioning look in his eyes. "Go!" I said. And he left without a word.

"First time I ever got orders from a coachman," said one of the guards, near enough to see my uniform.

"And it won't be the last," I said to him. "Go about your business."

I walked briskly away from them, and up the flight of stone steps that led into the heart of the Palace. I watched for the black cat, but there was no sign of it. Instead, there were people—running, laughing, stamping, spitting . . .

In Amadea's room there was already a crowd, but I was tall enough to see over and right to the back of the room where Devlin stood. He was beside an open cupboard, and was throwing dresses to the grasping hands.

"Princess, she was!" cried Devlin. "Silk dresses, while ordinary folk froze in rags. Here, take this, and this, and this!"

Each gift was greeted with cheers and more laughter. Some of the dresses were torn as the different pairs of hands tugged in different directions Devlin mocked on until there were no more dresses to throw except—produced from the very depths of the cupboard—something carefully wrapped in silver paper.

"What have we got here?" asked Devlin. "Another little treasure extracted from the sweat of the people?"

He unwrapped it slowly, to heighten the suspense, but when he finally held it up, there was a moment of surprised silence. In his hand was the ragged dress she had worn when I had first seen her in the kitchen.

"Well well," said Devlin. "Crown of gold and feet of clay. Who wants some rags for cleaning?"

"I do," I said, and all the heads turned to look at me.

"You want the rags, coachman?" said Devlin.

"They'll look good on my horses," I said.

People laughed, and the dress was passed back from hand to hand until it reached me.

"Thank you, Mr. Devlin," I called. "If you need a coachman, I'm your man, sir!"

"I'll remember that," he said. "Now, let's see what else the royal family has to offer us."

I did not wait to watch the desecration. There were other things for me to do, and I made my way against the incoming tide of people until at last I was out on the stone steps again. The Prince's naked body was still there, the head twisted grotesquely in the huge stain of blood. Some men were standing nearby.

"Give me a hand with the body," I said. "It's to be loaded on to the coach."

They did not want to obey me, but I moved and spoke with authority, as if they had no choice.

"Be careful with the head," I said. "One of you support it."

We carried the body down the steps, and I laid my cloak on the floor of the coach to receive it. Then I thanked the men, and they walked away, believing they had done right. I climbed into my seat, and drove slowly across to the pyre, which was now merely black and smouldering. What had once been Amadea was a shadow.

There were a few people still at the pyre, and as I drew near I was startled to recognize the two sisters and their mother. They stood ashen-faced, gazing at the charred ruins. I got down from the coach, and approached them.

"Was she a witch?" I asked.

"If the people say she was a witch," said the mother, "then she was a witch."

"She would have had us killed, then," whispered one of the sisters.

"Hold your tongue, girl," said the mother.

"What's he got there?"

The other sister had noticed the dress that I was still carrying over my arm.

"Where did you get that?" asked the mother, with an edge of both anger and fear in her voice.

"Mr. Devlin gave it to me," I said. "It belonged to the Princess. Now stand aside. I have to take the remains and burry her."

I stepped carefully onto the smouldering boards and branches, in order to reach the shadow at the top. I could scarcely bear to look at it. A rat would not have known such horror, but rats neither suffer nor inflict as men do. I caught up the cindered bundle, and descended.

"Where are you taking her?" asked the mother.

"To a place where she can rest in peace," I said. "Away from your world."

I brushed past them, and returned to my coach. There I laid Amadea down on the seat, above the body of her Prince, and as I straightened, something landed with a metallic chink on the floor. It was a purse. I turned and saw the three women walking slowly away, but did not trouble to throw it after them.

I set my horses into a swift gallop, wanting only to take my two precious shells as fast as possible away from this Golgotha. I did not know where we were heading, but the horses knew, and we raced out of the town, up into the hills. At last they halted at a spot that seemed already to have been chosen. There was forest all around, but from this particular place one could see the great dome of the sky, and the sweep of the hills and fields, while the town lay far and tiny like a child's puzzle in the distance. You could not imagine walls or crowds in this place, for the air was sweet and the only sound was bird-song.

On the ground lay a sharp, hollowed stone, and with this I dug the grave in which I laid the flakes and bones of Amadea and the pale twisted body of her husband. When at last the work was done, I set a simple cross of two branches in the earth, and then knelt down beside it.

"Now I have buried you," I said, "and they'll not touch you again. But for him who severed you from me and from this life, there'll be punishment. I swear to you that I shall never rest until Devlin dies, and dying, knows why he dies. Now Prince and gentle Princess, lie here in peace until the world's end."

XVII

By the time I reached the town again, it was dark night. My horses had found the way for me, for I should certainly have got lost in the hills. As we drew near to the Palace, the sounds of music came piercing through the night. It was not the sweet rhythms of that first ball; nor was it the alluring lilt of Jenkins' recorder—no, this music was strident and jangling, with shrilling pipes and harsh, metallic drums. The whole area in front of the Palace was lit up with a thousand torches, and people were dancing, singing, drinking. A clown stood on Amadea's pyre, emitting mock shrieks of agony, and the mob roared with laughter, and applauded the spectacle. Why? I could see no cause for laughter or applause in this.

Suddenly a cheer went up from the front, and it was soon taken up all around, swelling like an approaching storm. Hands were waved in the air, and the voices took up a chant: Devlin, Devlin, Devlin. He had come out on to the steps—and I noticed that the golden gate was leaning crazily on its hinges behind him. On the wall—black on white—someone had scrawled the words: 'People's Palace'. Devlin, Devlin, Devlin. Devlin was accompanied by guards, amongst whom I recognized John standing close to him. The friends who had been on the platform were also there with him, though they and the guards stood discreetly behind, so that Devlin alone could be the focus. Devlin, Devlin, Devlin.

I left my coach, and mingled with the raving crowd. Devlin held up his hand, and the storm subsided. The great man was to speak.

"Fellow citizens," he cried, "fellow victors, fellow rulers." Another cheer erupted, but he raised his hand again to still the roar.

"This is the greatest day in the history of our country. Together we have destroyed tyranny and witchcraft, and in its place we have established a true government of the people. There'll be nobody homeless, nobody starving, nobody poor in this new land of ours. And there'll be no rich princes, no slave-driving landowners, no oppressors of the meek. This is now the land of freedom and of opportunity. Will you help me to make it work?"

"Yes!" howled the mob.

"Is it what you want?"

"Yes!"

"Will you accept me as leader?"

"Yes!"

"Or do you want the Prince and the witch to return?"

"No!"

"Then listen, my people!" cried Devlin. "We will serve you, every minute of every day, and there'll be no man—that I promise—who will look back on this day with anything but pride. And one day you'll tell your grandchildren that you were there, that you were present and helping, when Devlin overthrew the tyrant and set up a rule of peace and plenty. Go home now, my friends, my fellow rulers, go home and tonight sleep the sleep of triumph. There's much to be done, but together—you and I—we shall succeed!"

How they cheered. The mouths spread so wide that they seemed to swallow their faces. Perhaps, too, they had swallowed their brains. What did these fools know about Devlin? And what did they know about the goodness they had destroyed? No animal, said my father, can destroy as man can. And yet, said my father, you can outthink him and feed off him. Of course he could be outthought, for he was clumsy and he was gullible, and he wanted to follow and would follow the one who would lead. Wide the mouths, and loud the voices, and the air was heavy with liquored breath. Devlin, they cried, Devlin, Devlin. And a day ago they would have cried "Long live the Prince and Princess!"

As I stood in the midst of that vicious and mindless crowd, I knew suddenly what I had been born to do. Kill Devlin, yes, as I had already sworn to do. But Devlin was only for personal revenge—the stone of satisfaction within the wall of duty. My task was to shatter the whole wall. Every one of these triumph-screaming mouths must one day scream with fear and the pain of death, such as they had inflicted upon *her*. And upon my father, and upon every one of my fellows that had died at their hands. What were they doing upon the earth? Did not every creature tremble because of them, and yet what greatness did they restore to the earth in exchange for their power? None. Destruction, only destruction. Then let them be destroyed, and let the world go its way without them.

Devlin, Devlin, Devlin, they cried. And he smiled, and he waved, and he mouthed to his friends who smiled. I had now pushed my way close enough to see those stiff whiskers twitching as he smiled, and I saw that he was standing on a box which gave him more height of authority. He raised both arms to acknowledge the cheers, and the gesture brought forth an even greater roar. A man next to me dug me in the ribs and said: "Greatest day of our lives, eh?"

"It's a day of ending," I said, and he nodded uncomprehendingly before turning towards Devlin again and resuming the worship. But a day of ending it would be. In their ignorance and cruelty they had ended the true order, and now I would outthink them to end their very existence. I had become a human being. And on this, my first day, I had learned to weep, I had learned to lie, and I had learned to hate. Already I knew how to plan and how to kill. Soon I should be the angel of their destruction.

The bell struck. Involuntarily I began to count, and for some reason those near me took up the count, which spread across the whole crowd: One, two, three, four, five, six, seven, eight, nine, ten, eleven, twelve. It was midnight. Suddenly I was rigid with apprehension. I tried to see my coach and horses, but the dense crowd had blocked them from my view. Everyone was cheering again, but still I waited . . . Rat or man? Man or rat? . . . I did not change. The woman of light had imposed no condition. I would stay a man, and they would all live to rue it.

Devlin had sent the guards down amongst the crowd to make everyone go home. Yet they could not see that as 'fellow rulers' they had the right to stay. "Go on home," said the guards, and the people obeyed. But I stood my ground, for I was a man and I was more than their equal.

"He's the one, Mr. Devlin!" cried a shrill voice. "That's him over there!"

"The coachman?" I heard Devlin say.

"Yes, he took away the bodies, I'm sure of it!"

"Guards!" called Devlin. "Seize that man, and bring him to me!"

And drawing their swords, three guards converged upon me.

XVIII

"**P**ut your swords down," I said, and I strode past them and up the steps. So certain was my gait that not one of them dared to block my way.

"I would have come to see you anyway, Mr. Devlin," I said.

"You took her rags and then you took her body," said Devlin.

"Hers and the Prince's," I said, "but only in your service, sir."

"What do you mean?" asked Devlin.

He had got off his box now, and I towered above him. Until this moment I had not realized how very small he was. Yet his smallness gave me no feeling of security—on the contrary, it made him seem more dangerous. There was light in the tiny eyes behind the spectacles, and the light was sharper than a tooth.

"What do you mean, in my service?" he asked again.

"When I came near the Prince's body, sir," I said, "there were men and women all round. They were gazing on the body, and they were inspired to pity, not hatred. I heard them asking aloud if what had been done was right. And when the flames died down round the burnt Princess, I heard more questionings. The sight of death can change belief to doubt. And so I deemed it wise to remove the causes of the doubt. I've buried them where no-one will find them. Without a body, sir, there is no martyrdom."

Devlin listened to me in silence, his eyes never leaving my face.

"Do I know you, coachman?" he said at length.

"You will have seen me, sir," I replied. "I am your follower."

"There's something about you," said Devlin. "But not the face . . ."

"Did I do well, sir?" I asked.

"Yes," said Devlin. "You're clearly a man of enterprise. I shall need followers like you."

"You have only to command, sir," I said.

"But where have I seen you? What's your name?"

"People merely call me Coachman, sir. I should deem it an honour were you to do the same."

"Very well, Coachman. There is a service you can do me. In the morning, collect two of my men and they'll take you to my lodgings. I want you to bring all my belongings here—in particular all my papers."

"You'll be living in the Palace?" I asked.

"Of course," he said.

Of course. Where else would he live? If you take their lives, why should you not take their house as well? And their wealth and their power, and ultimately their title?

"I shall do it gladly, sir," I said. "But I shall not need your men."

"To help you load . . ." he said.

"I am strong enough to dig graves, sir," I said. "Your affairs will be here tomorrow morning."

"But you don't know where I live."

"I know it, sir."

I told him the exact address. Still he could not read me to his satisfaction, and the brilliant eyes studied my face. I did not flinch.

"You seem to doubt me, sir," I said.

"No, no," he replied hastily. "But you remind me of someone, that's all."

"I shall be here in the morning, sir, with your affairs."

"Thank you, Coachman."

"But I shall need your key, sir."

"Yes, of course."

He gave me the key, and I half bowed to him before turning away. As I left, I heard someone ask: "Are you sure you can trust him?" Devlin's reply pleased me: "I'd rather have such a man inside than outside."

I drove straight to Devlin's lodgings, pausing only to look at the house next door. It was in darkness. For me it would always be in darkness, but that was no longer my concern. I descended Devlin's steps, and unlocked the door. When my eyes had accustomed themselves to the gloom, I began to stack his papers together and to carry them out to the coach. Although it was late, I was used to working at night, and I wanted the morning for other things.

I had been in and out three times when a light shone in a ground-floor window. I saw the light move through the room and out into the hall, and then the front door opened and an old woman stood in the doorway.

"Mr. Devlin?" she called.

"No," I said. "Mr.Devlin is at the Palace. He sent me to collect his affairs."

She came down the front steps—a shrivelled creature in a white night-dress, holding her taper aloft as she picked her way towards me.

"Is it true he had the Prince killed?" she asked.

"It's true," I said.

"And *he's* to be Prince?"

"He's going to rule us. No doubt eventually he'll name himself Prince."

"Then I shall have to take care, only he owes me six months' rent. How am I going to ask him? I live on my rent, you see. I only have the house and the rent, I've nothing else. He owes me six months' rent, and he promised he would pay me."

"I'll tell him."

"What am I going to do if he doesn't pay?"

At first I felt sorry for her, but now she began to insist, and to pluck at my sleeve with her bony fingers, as if she could dig her rent out of me.

"I've got nothing else," she moaned. "How am I going to get the rent from him?"

I grasped her wrist firmly, and forced her arm down to rest by her side.

"I'll tell him," I said again.

"He won't pay me," she said.

I suddenly thought of the purse that had been tossed from heavy consciences into my coach.

"Wait," I said, and left her reaching for the air. I took a handful of coins from the purse, and brought them back to her.

"Will this cover it?" I asked.

I saw her eyes open wide, and knew that it was more than enough. But then the eyes narrowed again, and she looked from the coins to me and then back to the coins again.

"Six months he owes me," she said. "Six whole months."

I fetched some more coins, and she could barely contain a laugh of greed. Then without another word, she hobbled back up the steps, clutching her coins, and almost falling over herself in her eagerness to be indoors and counting them.

I worked till the coach was full, and then I sat in one of Devlin's chairs, draped my cape around me, and slept till first light. I could have used his bed, but I would have felt too close to him there.

When the sun woke me, I took an apple from Devlin's food cupboard, and then hastened to the coach. I had a great deal to do this morning before I went to the Palace. I drove past Amadea's house, but there was no sign of movement. Part of me longed to go into the house, perhaps because part of me felt that she was still there, and even that I was still there. But I drove on.

My first call was to Jenkins' house. When he opened his door, there was a look of bewilderment and fear on his face.

"Let me in, please," I said, and pushed past him into the room.

"It was you who rescued me," he said.

"Do you not know who I am?" I asked.

He looked hard and long at me. The fear had gone—no doubt he had half expected to be arrested again, but my bearing had reassured him. Now, though, I could see the idea behind his eyes, and the reluctance to express it through his lips.

"Are you . . . Rob . . .?"

He could not even finish the name.

"Yes," I said. "They changed me back."

He threw his arms round me, and for some reason the gesture brought tears into my eyes.

"Robert, Robert," he said, "my good Robert, my brave Robert!"

She had called me brave, too. And there was something of her in him.

"What's to become of us all?" he said. "If they can kill the Prince and Princess like that, what will they do next?"

"They won't survive," I said.

He looked uncertainly at me.

"What makes you say that?" he asked.

"Because they have an enemy."

"You? But what can you do?"

"Devlin turned this world upside down," I said. "And I am stronger than Devlin."

Again a look of fear came into his eyes, but I spoke before he could ask me his question.

"I need to study some books," I said. "Will you let me stay to read them?"

"As long as you like," he said. "But this is not a safe place, for either of us. When you knocked, I was afraid . . ."

"I'm on an errand for Devlin," I said. "He's moving into the Palace. I shall arrange for you to take his rooms—he'll never think of looking for you there. You'll have to grow a beard, and change your name. Then you'll be safe. As for the books, I know what I want to read, and it won't take long. But I have to hurry, because he'll be expecting me."

Jenkins gestured that I was free to read what I liked, and as I settled down to the books, he made coffee for us both. When it was ready, he brought it to the table, and he sat in silence watching me. In reality, I was not so much reading as searching, and when eventually I found the passage that I dimly remembered, I studied it and dwelt upon it.

"I didn't know you were so interested in ancient history," said Jenkins, peering across my shoulder. I closed the book.

"The triumph of human culture," I said. "The past is always there for us to learn from. Now listen to me, Jenkins. When the time comes, I shall call for you and you must be ready to leave with me. I don't mean your removals—that we shall attend to tomorrow. What I'm planning will take many weeks, perhaps months, but you must always be prepared to go."

"Robert, Robert, what terrible thing is in your mind?"

"Better for you not to know," I said. "Now I must leave you."

"Robert, be careful of Devlin. Traitors are not easily betrayed."

"Devlin was a good teacher, if nothing else," I said. "In one day he taught me more than a hundred books. But I'll be careful of him. And I shan't make your mistake."

"My mistake?"

"Putting heart and tongue together. Devlin will only hear from me what he wants to hear."

He stood looking at me with those troubled eyes, and I allowed him to ask just one of the many questions written there.

"Where did you learn to hate like this, Robert?"

"In front of the Palace," I said. "When from your hand I saw them take off the Prince's head and burn the Princess. I shall help you to move house tomorrow. And I have a favour to ask of you."

"You may ask anything. I owe you my life."

"Will you teach me to play the recorder?"

His eyes registered a surprised disbelief, but then he saw that I was serious. "Of course," he said, "if that's what you want."

"It's essential for me," I said. "We'll talk about it again tomorrow."

I left him, for I was anxious to accomplish my other tasks. My second call was to the instrument-maker. From him I bought a recorder.

My third call was to the apothecary. From him I bought a jar of poison. I told him it was for rats.

XIX

It was mid-morning when I reached the Palace. The remains of the pyre had been removed, and there were four guards outside the golden gate, which had been repaired. Behind them, the crudely written 'People's Palace' had been wiped off, and instead the same words were printed on an ornate sign. There were a few sightseers, but they kept away from the Palace itself, and mine was the only coach to be seen. The quietness was eerie after the shattering din of the previous day. Could it all have been a dream?

No sooner had I stopped the coach at the foot of the steps than two soldiers with drawn swords were demanding to know my business there.

"I've brought Mr. Devlin's affairs," I said, and dismounted. "You're to help me carry them inside."

They looked uncertainly at each other, and called to a colleague.

"I'll ask the captain," he said, and the golden door was opened to admit him.

"Help me unload," I commanded the first two soldiers. They did as they were told, and we began to take Devlin's belongings out of the coach and to pile them on the steps.

The guard returned.

"It's all right," he said. "It's to be taken to Mr. Devlin's rooms."

"You'd better take me to Mr. Devlin himself," I said, "and in the meantime get your colleagues to carry these things."

"Mr. Devlin's in conference at the moment," said the guard.

"I'm acting under his instructions," I said. "Take me to him."

The guard took me into the Palace and up a flight of stairs. We came to a corridor which was full of soldiers, all of whom were standing in silence outside the tall closed doors of the conference room. John was one of the soldiers, though he was wearing a different, more elaborate uniform now. At my approach it was he who came forward, authoritatively laying his fingers on his lips to ensure there was no noise.

"He wants to see Mr. Devlin," whispered my companion.

"You'll have to wait," said John. "And don't make a sound."

From inside the conference room I could hear Devlin's high, piercing voice:

". . . a basis of power. How can we govern when we're not safe?"

"But the people are with us!" said a voice.

110

"For how long?" said Devlin. "The people are fickle. They'll expect miracles, and when no miracles come they'll grow restless. Now is the time to establish control, when the people believe in us."

"What sort of control are you talking about, Devlin?"

"A well equipped army of a thousand men. If the Prince had had a thousand men at his command, do you think we'd have overthrown him? With a force of that strength, we can overwhelm all opposition. Even now there are voices raised against us. I have it on reliable authority that some people were standing over the Prince's body questioning whether his death had been right."

"But where's the money to come from, to pay for this army?"

"We shall have to raise taxes."

"No, no, the reforms must come first."

"Safety must come first!" cried Devlin. "The basis of power is force. Besides, with an army of a thousand men, our sights need not be confined to this town alone. I don't intend to be trammelled here."

Several voices were now raised in protest. John lifted his hand, and the guards stiffened in readiness.

"That's not what the revolution was for!" cried one voice.

"The people won't pay!" shouted another.

"Reform! Reform!"

But above these cries rang the high-pitched summons of Devlin himself: "Guards! Arrest these men!"

John and the soldiers burst into the conference room, and through the open door I watched them seize every one of the men that sat or stood at the long table. Devlin himself was sitting at the head, calmly watching the brief and unequal struggle.

"What do you want done with them, sir?" asked John.

"Take them to the dungeons, captain," said Devlin. "They'll think more clearly down there."

Amongst the prisoners was the man in the black gown.

"You have laid hands of violence upon the Church!" he said to Devlin. "You'll be punished by heaven if not by earth!"

"I'll take that risk," said Devlin, "since both seem to be on my side at the moment."

The prisoners were taken away, but John remained behind. Devlin rose to his feet and clasped John's hand.

"Well done, Captain John!" he said, barely containing his excitement. "Now you and I have full control of government and people. The race is to the swift."

He suddenly caught sight of me in the corridor.

"What is it, Coachman?" he asked.

I entered the room.

"Forgive me, sir," I said. "I didn't wish to disturb you, but there are matters for which I need your approval."

"Yes?"

"I've brought most of your belongings, and the rest I shall bring on a second journey. Your landlady importuned me for six months' rent, and I paid her in your name. Was this right?"

He laughed his dry smile-less laugh. "You needn't have bothered," he said, "but I'll see you're reimbursed."

"I don't ask for payment, sir," I said. "I merely wanted to ensure you were not being robbed."

My solicitude surprised him, and the tiny eyes widened a little, but my surface was solid.

"To avoid trouble, I've arranged for another tenant to take your place. When I arrived at the Palace with your belongings this morning, I was challenged and threatened with drawn swords. I should be grateful for a guarantee of safety when I next come."

"Of course," he said. "Captain, please ensure that our coachman is given safe passage at all times."

"Yes, sir," said John.

"I have one more favour to ask you," I said. "My horses will need provender, and if we are to serve you, then they and I will need to be accommodated. May we use and stay in the Palace stables?"

"With pleasure," he said. "But you need not stay in the stables yourself. Inform the domestic staff on my authority that you are to be given a room here in the Palace."

"Thank you, sir," I said. "You are most generous."

"Is there anything else?" he asked.

"No, sir," I said. "I must go and supervise the unloading of your belongings."

I half-bowed to him, and left.

Devlin had chosen for himself the Prince's own apartment—large, richly appointed rooms which seemed grotesquely defiled by the dirty boxes and papers now being stowed within.

"These things are to be placed neatly, not strewn around," I said to the soldiers.

Their reactions were hostile, but not one dared to defy me, and the boxes and papers were put in some order.

Thus I had earned permanent access to the Palace, had established some authority over the guards, and had gained the trust of Devlin himself.

I duly brought the rest of Devlin's belongings, and the next day I helped Jenkins to move to his new lodgings. The old woman was greatly relieved to have a new tenant so soon. We told her that his name was Jones, and I made sure that he did not pay her the rent she first demanded.

For the next few weeks, I served Devlin faithfully. I was always on hand when he needed transport, and I took upon myself the task of supervising the domestic and kitchen staff. I ensured that Mr. Devlin's rooms were kept spotlessly clean, that his meals were cooked as and when he liked them, that his clothes were washed and his sheets changed, that no-one disturbed him when he did not wish to be disturbed—I was discreet, I was efficient, I was dependable, I was indispensable.

I had only one moment of embarrassment, very early on in my rise to indispensability: the serving-maid whom I had kissed at the ball was still employed in the kitchen, and she recognized me. At least, she thought she recognized me. I naturally disclaimed all knowledge of her, told her brusquely that I had been nowhere near the Palace on that occasion, and warned her against daring to assume the slightest degree of familiarity. She apologized for her mistake, and thenceforth kept her place.

I left the Palace only with the express assurance of Devlin himself that he would not be needing me. On such occasions, I would drive into the town to take my recorder lessons with Jenkins. He was puzzled by my eagerness, but impressed by my progress, for in no time I had mastered the basic technique of the instrument and was able to play the melodies he had shown me. The rest was a matter of feeling and control, and these came more slowly.

In the town itself, there were increasing numbers of soldiers. Devlin had set about recruiting young men, and had established a training camp for them in the grounds of the Palace. They were not allowed, however, to enter the Palace—this privilege was reserved for an exclusive group of the old guards who were under the command of Captain John. They were even given different uniforms and were called The Palace Guards, as distinct from The Army, which title covered all the remaining soldiers. Occasionally in the town I would see the tax-collectors. In the past they had gone about their business quietly and unobtrusively, but now they were always accompanied by at least two soldiers, armed with heavy swords.

Devlin had, of course, been right in his assessment of the people. Their initial enthusiasm for the new government waned rapidly, and when the taxes were increased to pay for the new army, there was much discontent. In vain did Devlin send his men round the town to point out to the taxpayers that he was looking after their safety. "Looking after our money, more like it!" was the typical response. But he had been careful to engage and train his soldiers *before* raising the taxes. He also employed men to mix with the people and find out where the most dangerous opponents were to be found. These he had removed (usually at dead of night)—at first to the Palace dungeons, but when these became overcrowded, he took over a thick-walled house in the town, and kept them locked in there. The arrests were carried out with ruthless efficiency and with total disregard for the customary trappings of justice. There were never any trials.

It was some three months after Devlin had seized power that the first reports began to reach the Palace of animals dying mysteriously in the town. The only animals affected were cats and dogs, but on several occasions they had been found dead in the streets—usually in the mornings, though sometimes even in the afternoons and evenings. Their bodies were always stiff and their teeth clenched, as though they had died in considerable pain. There was a good deal of concern in the Palace when the disease was found to have reached there as well. Cats and dogs began to die at an alarming rate, and indeed so swift was the spread of the epidemic that before long the Palace was entirely free of those animals.

As there was no part of the Palace to which I did not have continual access, it was easy for me to poison the animals' food. And on my frequent visits to town, all I had to do was toss a poisoned titbit to some stray cat or dog, and then pick it up again when it had done its work. I would dispose of the evidence when crossing the bridge on the way back to the Palace. I would then join the servants or the guards, bringing them news of the latest outbreak, and speculating with them on the possible causes of these strange deaths.

One day I was discussing the mystery with the black-bearded guard who had taken off the Prince's head for the price of a suit of clothes and a coronet.

"Peculiar that it only strikes cats and dogs," he was saying.

"Pray heaven," I rejoined, "that we humans will never fall victim."

But a human was to fall victim.

XX

I had taken to breaking my fast with the guards, who had a dining-room of their own near the kitchen. We were sitting there together one morning when suddenly, without warning, the man with the black beard—the very same man I had talked to only recently—rose to his feet, clutching his throat and groaning in apparent agony. He soon fell to the floor, and while the rest of us stood by helplessly, he twitched, gasped, and finally died before our very eyes. Immediately after, another guard that had sat beside him screamed and clutched his throat, only to die in identical fashion.

Armed with the news of this latest appalling development, I immediately went to Devlin's apartment.

Breathlessly I informed him of the death of my two colleagues, and then I explained to him the terrible truth that lay behind this gruesome event:

"I have seen it before, sir," I said. "It was some years ago, in my own home town. Things began in the same way—dogs and cats found dead and dying. Then suddenly, unaccountably, the disease struck human beings as well. If we don't take measures urgently, we shall all be killed."

"What measures *can* we take?" he asked.

"Many people died in my town," I said, "but most were saved by . . . but the measure is a drastic one, sir."

"What measure, man, what measure?"

"We slaughtered all the cats and dogs. They're the carriers, you see. Without them, the disease must die out."

"Coachman, is this true?"

"My father, sir, was victim to this disease. I have good reason to tell you the truth."

Devlin frowned as he deliberated.

"The cats and the dogs will be no loss. And we have the men to carry out the slaughter. Coachman, you've done us good service this day. If your method works, we shall all stand in your debt."

"The order must be carried out swiftly, sir. Every moment puts us in greater peril."

He gave the order. And that same day the soldiers went into town, their swords drawn. I drove in myself, to supervise the slaughter, and the roads ran red with the blood of the cats and dogs. Some people wept, some complained, and some uttered warnings of evil consequences, but the killing continued. The next day we went out again, to ensure that no cat or dog had escaped. The soldiers dug trenches in which to bury the bodies, and I the coachman rat watched these final rites from my coach and gave no outward sign of my triumph.

Two more guards died, and in the town the bodies of two beggar men were found one morning, stiff and with teeth clenched. But after that, no more deaths. Days went by, a week, two weeks.

Devlin sent for me.

"Are we safe?" he asked.

"When was the last death?"

"Two weeks ago."

"Then, sir, we are safe. But let no more dogs or cats be brought to this town for a year, to ensure the final passing of the disease."

The deliverance of the town was a cause for celebration, and when Devlin had the townspeople informed of the success of his measures, he was given due credit. Even those who had grumbled at the rise in taxes, and those who had bewailed the loss of their cats and dogs—all were forced to admit that he had handled the crisis well. The people were grateful to Devlin, and Devlin was grateful to me. Not only had I presented him with the means of salvation, but I had also kept quiet about my advisory role, leaving him to claim the credit and the glory.

Throughout this time I had continued my work with the recorder, and by now I was as proficient as Jenkins himself. Indeed he believed that I had exceeded his skill, for he detected in my playing an appeal that even he could not match. I now played melodies of my own, some of which he said seemed almost to draw him out of his skin, such was the quality of their message and the delicacy of their tone.

"You are an artist," he said to me one evening. "You've come here to teach me, for in truth I have nothing left to teach you."

He was right. I could do what I liked with the instrument—it was no longer separate but was truly an extension of myself. The time had come, however, for me to test this skill, and it was with no little apprehension that I put my recorder to my lips as I drove home that night. The streets were deserted—as was usual at that time—and the notes brought forth a strange echo from the walls of the houses. At first this was the only sound, but soon I noticed a rustling, and shadows moved. As I played, I glanced behind, and again I caught movements—difficult to discern but palpable. I stopped playing, and the movements stopped, and the shadows were still. I was satisfied.

Before I had left Jenkins that night, I had warned him that the time would soon come when I would call to take him away, and I reminded him always to be ready to leave. He pressed me to tell him more, but I would not. Now with my recorder on the seat beside me, I knew with mounting excitement that I would indeed soon have my revenge on Devlin and on this whole town, and when I reached the Palace I could barely restrain myself from going straight to Devlin's room. But I did restrain myself, for the nearest town was a day's ride away, and if my plan was to work, it was best that I should arrive there only at night. I knew that Devlin had no appointments for the following day, and so I waited with impatience for morning to come.

On the day of the executions, Devlin had woken me when the sun had barely begun to rise. The day now dawning was to be as momentous, and so I repaid him in kind. The night had just started to lift when I stole to his apartment, and let myself in.

XXI

Devlin was still asleep. Gently I shook him. He awoke with a start.

"What? What is it? Coachman? My glasses!"

I handed them to him.

"What is it, Coachman? What time . . ."

"Sir," I said, in an urgent whisper, "forgive me for this intrusion, but your life is in danger."

"My life?" he echoed, sitting up in his bed, face as pale as his nightshirt.

"There's a plot against you. The guards. They plan to overthrow you. We have no time to lose."

"What plot? Why?"

"Please, Mr. Devlin, sir, I beg you, get dressed as quickly as you can. I'm risking my life to save you."

I helped him to put on his clothes. His body was almost skeletal. How could such damage be inflicted by so small and puny a frame? He had commanded, conquered, killed, and yet even a dog could have knocked him over and torn him apart.

"What plot are you talking about? Who's plotting?"

"Last night I overheard Captain John and some of the guards. They plan to kill you and to take over the government themselves. But I have a way to foil them. Now please listen to me. My home town is one day's ride from here. I have many friends there, and I can raise a force that will easily be strong enough to overcome the Palace Guards. But you must do as I say."

"How can you raise a force . . .?"

"Listen, sir, please! As far as I know, it's only the guards that are involved. The Army would probably follow whoever came out victorious. That will be us. Now we'll leave here and go straight to my coach. If we meet any guards on the way, you must say that you're driving with me into town, but that you'll be back later in the day. That way they'll suspect nothing, and do nothing."

"But John wouldn't turn against me."

"You don't know him. John is ambitious. And he's envious. And he's got them to follow him. Are you ready, sir?"

Had he at this moment called for the guards or for Captain John, I should certainly have lost my life, but how could he call for them? I was his trusted servant, and I had allowed him no time for thought. Survival—for man as for rat. He was afraid.

I took him along the corridor and down the steps that led to the dungeons.

"Why this way?" he whispered.

"The back way is safer," I said. "My coach is in the stable."

Most of the prisoners were asleep in the dungeons, but one was up against the bars and heard our coming. In the gloom I could not see who it was, but he called out to us that he was sick and we should have mercy on him. His hand tugged at my cape as I went past.

"Prisoner," I said to him, "death comes no harder for prisoners than for princes. Wait patiently."

There was a guard outside the door. When he saw who we were, he snapped to attention.

"I'm taking Mr. Devlin into town," I said. "We shall return shortly."

I strode two or three paces ahead of Devlin, who now ran to catch up with me.

"Wait, Coachman!" he said. "I can take a troop of soldiers into the Palace and confront John . . ."

"The Captain would deny everything," I said. "Besides, I can't be sure how many of the soldiers are with him. Mr. Devlin . . ."

I stopped and faced him now.

". . . Mr. Devlin, I have served you faithfully ever since the day you saved our town from tyranny, but I have never served you better than this day. I beg of you to accompany me now, but if you wish to stay, I must ask you to release me from my post. I don't wish to die, and I don't wish to see you die."

"All right, Coachman," he said, "I'll come with you."

We reached the stable. He wanted to ride with me, but I made him get into the coach.

"It has to look normal, sir," I said. "Remember, the guards believe we're driving into town."

And so we rode out of the Palace yard and away down the tree-lined avenue. But we did not cross the bridge. Instead we took the road that ran beside the river and that would lead us eventually to the next town. When we were out of sight of the Palace, Devlin leaned out of the window and called to me to stop, so that he could come and ride beside me. I pretended not to hear him, and left him to make of that what he would.

But eventually I had to stop, to give the horses rest and refreshment. Devlin climbed out of the coach.

"I kept calling to you to stop," he said angrily. "Didn't you hear me?"

"Forgive me, sir," I said, "It's impossible to hear noises above the horses' hooves. If I'd heard I would have stopped."

As so often before, his eyes shone into mine, trying to find out their secret, but I returned his gaze with total honesty.

"I have brought food, sir," I said. "If you would not mind sharing a meal with me."

We sat on the grass.

"You're a strange fellow," he said. "Why do you serve me so faithfully?"

"Some are born to lead, some are born to follow," I said. "But the follower must choose his leader well."

"Why did you choose to follow me?"

"Because you have the strength and the courage to give us a new world. You don't hold back when obstacles arise. Emotion, sentiment, they never interfere with your judgement. You're a man who knows what he wants, and will not be stopped from attaining it. Such a man I will serve faithfully."

"What do you hope to get out of it?"

"To play my part. To be valuable to a great man."

He was silent for a moment. I could see that he was pleased. But then his expression clouded again.

"When did you overhear this plot?"

"It was during the night, sir. I had stabled my horses, and was on my way to my room when I heard voices from the conference chamber. Their plan was to enter your room, assassinate you, and take over power themselves, with John as leader."

"I trusted John!"

"A leader cannot afford to trust. A leader must depend on no-one but himself."

"When we return, I shall have him hanged by his heels. And the rest of them. Now, you must explain your plan to me. Who are these men you intend to bring back?"

"I have many brothers and many friends in the town we're going to. They're all warriors. With them on your side, you'll be able to hold any town at your command."

"How can you be sure they'll come with us?"

"They will obey me. More I cannot tell you, but you shall see for yourself when we arrive."

"It'll be night when we arrive."

"That is essential to my plan. Sir, we must leave now, but first may I make so bold as to ask you a question?"

"That much I certainly owe you," he said.

"Do you hate your fellow man, or do you love him?"

The question seemed both to amuse and to puzzle him. He thought about it for some time, and then said: "I feel nothing for my fellow man, neither love nor hate. Ideas are all that I care for."

XXII

We reached the outskirts of our destination before sunset, but it suited me to give the horses a long rest. Once we entered the town, we would not be able to stop again until we completed the return journey—which meant that we would be travelling right through the night. Devlin was now very restless. He had had plenty of time to think and he was becoming increasingly uncertain about the plot I claimed to have discovered and about the army I had promised to raise. He questioned me repeatedly about John and the guards, about my connections with this town, about the necessity for waiting till nightfall, about transport for the new army. I answered all his questions with patience and humility, never once allowing him the slightest glimpse of the truth.

"You say we shan't be able to stop once we've entered the town," he said. "I don't understand this. Are the people your enemies?"

"No, sir," I said. "But the army I shall raise is no ordinary army."

"Well?"

"We shan't be able to stop, sir."

"I know that. I want to know why."

"I don't wish to alarm you, sir, but if we stop, our lives may be in danger. The sun has now set, sir, and it's time for us to go."

"I shall ride with you, Coachman. I want to see this mystery for myself."

"Yes, sir."

It fitted in with my plans that he should ride with me. I could then restrain him if he should attempt to call for help or to jump off the coach. I helped him up into the seat, and we began a slow descent into the town. He was very nervous, and once even suggested that we should turn back.

"Sir," I said, "our heads are better on our shoulders that rolling down steps."

He shuddered and was quiet.

By the time we got into the town, the darkness was complete and, as I had expected, the streets were deserted. The lights shining from the windows were just sufficient to guide us, and I kept the horses in as straight a line as possible, so that we should be able to find our way back.

The town was much like our own, with narrow streets and broad squares. I wondered whether all towns were the same, and whether all the people that lived in them were the same too. Was there a Devlin here? Was there a Jenkins, a Prince, an Amadea? Had I been born in this town, would my life have been different? Was every destiny guided, or the mere whim of chance?

"Where are they, these soldiers of yours?" hissed Devlin.

"Everywhere," I said. "We must travel to the other side of the town and then summon them on our way back."

"How do you propose to summon them? And how are they going to travel?"

"They have their own means of transport," I said. "And they will respond to my signal."

When we had crossed the town, I turned the coach and stopped.

"What now?" asked Devlin.

I took my recorder from my cape.

"This is my signal," I said. "From now on, I shall not be able to speak to you. We shall travel without stopping, and you will jump from the coach at your peril."

"Why should I wish to jump from the coach?"

I did not answer, I put the recorder to my lips, and began to play, then with the instrument in my hands and the reins between my knees (for the horses needed little guidance from me), I set us on our return journey.

At first, nothing seemed to have changed. The streets still seemed deserted, and my music echoed from the walls of the houses as if in a hollow tube. But gradually I began to discern a rustling behind us, and the shadows around us began to flicker with movement. The rustling grew louder, until even Devlin could hear it above the rattle of hooves and wheels. He looked round, and he looked to the sides, and he peered ahead into the gloom.

"What's that noise? he asked.

But on we drove and on I played, and the noise grew louder, till it was like a wind and a rainstorm together, rushing and pattering, seething and pummelling . . .

"What is it?" screamed Devlin. "Coachman!"

Heads were thrust out of windows as we raced past, and the whole town must have been wakened by the pounding feet of my army.

"It's witchcraft!" cried Devlin.

It grew and grew, yet still my melodies pierced the storm, bringing more and more of my soldiers out into the streets to follow the coach and the coachman. Devlin was terrified. Louder and louder, redoubling from the walls which shook with the earthquake rumbling . . . Devlin covered his ears . . . We were a hurricane sweeping through the town, and I was the god of the wind and rain, master of the elements, playing the tune that could bring the whole world crashing down.

When at last Devlin made out the shapes of the moving shadows, his scream could emerge only as a hoarse whisper, though I heard it because I was waiting for it.

"Rats!" he cried. "Now I know who you are! Oh my God, I know who you are!"

XXIII

Once we were out of the town, the noise lessened as it spread across the fields. We slowed down, too, for the horses could never have kept up that furious gallop. The rats were now up with us, some scurrying alongside, the rest stretching out in a huge black shadow behind. Devlin had been silent ever since his discovery, but in any case he could have had no answers from me. There were times when the whistling and whirring of my soldiers seemed almost to be in harmony with my melodies, and I knew I could control my army totally.

There was an eerie joy in this ride. My enemy sat beside me, with no means of escape, and we were heading through the moonlit countryside towards the fulfilment of all my plans of destruction. I had become the monster that would outthink the monster, and in my choice of weapon was the sweetest irony imaginable. But know your enemy. Devlin was shrewd. He would not wait to die. He would realize that leaping from the coach would be fatal, as I should allow my army to devour him. He would in time work out that only one move could save him, and so I waited for him to make that move.

It came as we rode downhill—always the most difficult time for control. He suddenly stood and hurled himself at me, grasping with both hands for the recorder. If he could take it from me and hurl it away, I would lose control of the rats. But I did not let him take it from me. As he launched himself at me, I stood up, shook him back on to the seat, and still holding the recorder smashed my right hand into his face. He was no match for me, and the force of the blow made him whimper.

"My glasses!" he cried. "My glasses have gone!"

"If you try to attack me again," I said, "I'll throw you to the rats."

He scrabbled about our platform, looking for his glasses and whimpering. I raised my recorder to my lips and resumed playing.

He sat beside me after a while, feeling his face, but relapsing into silence again. Now we would be playing a strange game, for his silence was filled with desperate thoughts, and I had to guess those thoughts. Were I Devlin, what would I do? He knew we were heading back to our town, and he knew what the rats would do to the town. His prime concern, though, would be to save himself, not the town. Survival. He would have to talk. He would have to find out.

"If you want to kill me," he said, "why don't you kill me now?"

I enjoyed not answering.

"I can't escape from you," he said. "You may as well satisfy my curiosity."

I played on.

"All right," he said, "you intend to kill me at the place where I did my killing. Poetic justice. But these brothers of yours won't stop with me. They'll destroy the whole town. You have no quarrel with the town, have you? The town is full of innocent men, women, children . . . think of the children . . . You want them eaten alive? Why go into the town? Why not stop here and kill me?"

What did he care for the children?

"But you're clever," he said, "you know what you're doing. You know you're going to destroy the town. Of course, because you're a rat, not a man. I'd forgotten. Rats have no feelings. Rats are bodies without souls. Rats live only to eat. You have the form of a human, but Jenkins was right, you have no culture, no education, no fine feeling. You're a body, that's all."

Now I wanted to talk. Now I wanted to tell him about souls. Now I wanted to tell him about himself. I had to fight to keep the recorder between my lips, and the music became only half conscious.

"Men will always be superior to rats," he went on. "Even human rats like you. Because despite your cunning, you're without wisdom, without insight. Why, you would even have served a witch like Amadea because of her white hands and her blue eyes."

I stopped playing, and struck him again. My knuckles tore through the soft flesh and jarred against the bone. He almost fell from the seat, but hung on and righted himself.

"She was a whore, she was a witch, your Amadea. But a rat hasn't the intellect to see through such creatures. A rat can be lured even by a piece of cheese."

I was playing again, but I was playing badly. The twittering of my soldiers sounded angry, and the horses began to pull as if they were being bitten.

"You'll have to kill me to stop me talking, Coachman," he said, "and so long as I talk, I'll confront you with the truth you hate to hear."

I stopped the coach, I stopped playing, I stood and towered over him.

"Then I'll kill you now," I said.

He did not flinch.

"Go on, then," he said. "At least I shall have the pleasure of spoiling your perfect design. It'll be a poor revenge if you have to leave my dead body here, so far from your Amadea's pining ghost. Only a half-revenge for the half-human half-rat."

He was right. I wanted all.

Still I stood poised over him, undecided and needing time to unravel the possibilities. But he took the decision for me. With a sudden lunge, he seized not the recorder but the reins, and with a high-pitched yell he startled the horses into an immediate gallop. I was thrown off balance, and as I staggered, Devlin pushed me with all his might. I flew straight over the side of the coach, and crashed down on to the soft squirming bodies of my soldiers below. And the coach raced further and further away into the night till the darkness and distance swallowed it up. Devlin had escaped.

XXIV

The rats did me no harm. Devlin they would have eaten alive, but I was their kin, and I had known even as I fell that I was safe from their ravening.

The carpet of bodies had cushioned my fall, and apart from a few bruises I was unscathed. So too was my recorder, to which I had clung quite involuntarily. I picked myself up, while my soldiers milled at my feet as if impatient for their instructions. I stilled them with a few gentle notes which at the same time served to quieten my own anger and disappointment. These feelings I now had to banish totally. Devlin had out-thought me again, but to brood would have been futile. A new attack had to be planned, and nothing else mattered.

I enlivened the tune, and set my army on the march again. Every step was a step nearer to Devlin and revenge. We would march till we were tired, we would rest, then we would march again, and eventually we would descend upon the town and the Palace and devastate them. The excitement permeated through my melodics into my soldiers and they swarmed out in front of me like a relentless black tide. They hated men, and my revenge would be their revenge.

We marched through the night, and as the darkness began to lift I was able to see for the first time the true strength of this my army. There was no end to it. These soldiers were scurrying as far as the eye could see. They were not only on the road, but were racing across the fields on either side, and I knew that these fields would be left bitten and bare, for my soldiers were always hungry. As the light became brighter, I could even see dark clusters moving down from the hills to join the main flood—the country cousins were coming too! And when eventually we reached the town, we should double our force again. What could withstand such a power? I was almost glad that Devlin had escaped, so that I could savour the approaching moments all the more.

But my human body was now feeling the strain of my exertions. I had to rest. And so I summoned my soldiers off the road, and lulled them to stillness and silence. It seemed that I had only to think what I required, and it communicated itself to them directly through the music. Jenkins had once called music the purest expression of the soul, but he had also said it was for enjoyment and not for use. I knew better. This pure expression was a weapon with which to conquer the world.

I slept soundly, and would probably have slept right through the day had I not been awakened by a tugging and nipping at my legs and arms. The rats were communicating. I opened my eyes to a dazzle of green and blue and brown, but the rats had not woken me up so that I should admire the beauty of the day. In the distance, coming along the road that wound like a stream through the forested hills were six figures. They soon became clearer as men on horseback, and the glint of sun on metal showed that they were soldiers. They were already level with the advance guard of my army, but my soldiers lay still amongst the trees at the side. I gave low signals that they should all remain still, and the soldiers came on.

Obviously they had been sent by Devlin. He would have reached the Palace by daybreak, and would have wondered whether I had survived or not. These soldiers had the task of finding my body, or alternatively finding my army. But what could they do against us? Nothing. They would merely report back to Devlin, and he would make his plans accordingly.

On they came. How could they have failed to notice that the fields were brown instead of green? Surely they would look to the sides and not just to the front. Well, let them come. I would wait till they were level with me, then I would send in my troops to surround them. They would not report back to Devlin, and he would stay guessing and wondering.

They came level. But then, to my surprise, they veered off the road and galloped straight towards me. In a flash, I understood their tactics. Their mission was not to scout, it was to destroy me. Had they come six abreast, they would have succeeded, but they were riding single file, and that was their undoing. I sent my troops into action, and with a hundred bites at its fetlocks, the leading horse reared and threw off its rider. The other horses were blocked, and in no time all six horses and riders were down and covered by a seething mass of brown. I waded in amongst them, hoping to save one of the horses, but already it was too late. Animals and men had been killed instantaneously, and my army was gorging itself on the flesh. One thing alone I succeeded in rescuing. The second soldier had leapt off his horse and had fought bravely enough to gain a few extra seconds of life. I now cleared his body and removed the ragged remnants of his uniform. For all the tears and bloodstains, it was whole enough to be worn. I made a bag of my cape, folded the uniform and placed it inside the bag.

The speed at which horses and men were reduced to skeletons was astonishing. It was as if they had never had life or identity. Perhaps such feasting should have been obnoxious, but I had seen flesh consumed by fire because of hatred, and what I was now witnessing was no more hateful than a family gathering round a table for its evening meal. The flesh was good.

We had now covered about half the distance necessary, so that a non-stop march from here should bring us to our destination shortly before daybreak. This would be the ideal time for me to attack. And so we set out again, with my music sending rhythms of energy down into the legs of my willing soldiers. This was the easiest instruction, and I had no difficulty issuing it and maintaining it while another part of my brain engaged itself in planning.

The problem was to read Devlin's mind. I had underestimated him twice now, and a third failure could lose me everything. I must enter his head as I had entered the heads of people I had met in books. I must *become* Devlin.

The fact that he had sent his soldiers proved that he was not convinced I had died. He would hope for their return, but he would act on the assumption of the worst possibility. He would seek to protect himself. How do you protect yourself against an army of millions? He had shown me one way already: attack their leader. He would concentrate all his skill and all his strength on removing me. How? Could his soldiers not lie in wait for me, just as mine had waited for his? He would expect me to head for his Palace. Somewhere along the route to the

Palace, he would station a hundred, two hundred, five hundred men, all with the single purpose of killing me. "Let the rats go on," he would tell them. "Wait only for the coachman."

What about the town? His own safety would be paramount, but he would have to protect the town. A leader with no people is a head with no body. Besides, his ideas demanded the survival of the town. Then the attack must come well away from the town—many miles along the road, in order that the rats should not know where to head for. The road: that was the key. He would expect us to keep to the road. But supposing we were to cross the river, and approach the town from the other side? How could we? We had never lost sight of the river on our daylight coach ride yesterday, but there had been no bridges. Bridges were only to be found in towns, and there was nothing between here and there.

But that would be our advantage. He would never expect us to come from the other side. If we could get across the river, we would by-pass his men and descend on the town before anyone could have an inkling of our presence. There would be guards at the bridge, of course, but they would be for defence, not attack, and my forces could dispose of them if I did not do so myself by subterfuge. We had only to cross the river.

From now on we followed the river and not the road. My fear was that night might fall before we had found a suitable crossing-point, for the current flowed so fast that a night crossing would be hazardous. However, the sun was still high when I found what I had been looking for. The river narrowed and on its banks were trees that towered far into the sky. My orders slid through the trees, and my soldiers set to work with their fearsome tools, chewing, gnawing, cracking . . . Down came the first of the giants with an agonized creak and a final crash into the water. With its last layers of bark it clung to its roots, and the current swept it sideways back to the bank. But the next tree was tall enough, and its branches clung to the thick bushes on the other side. Another tree reached across, and then another, and all told some five or six fell to form our bridges. Then over we went, scrambling and scratching along precarious footholds above greedy waters . . . more and more came across, more and more, until at last the vast army was swirling through the fields on the other side of the river. I do not know how many we lost to the water, but the countryside was brown again with those that had survived the crossing. And so we made our way onwards through the evening, the twilight, the night, coming closer and closer to an unsuspecting town.

XXV

We veered right away from the river, and entered the town on the side furthest from the Palace. There was not a soldier in sight. It was still dark when we began our invasion, and soon the streets were echoing with the wind and the thunder of my army's voices and feet.

But Devlin had not abandoned his people altogether. I saw that doors and shutters had been tightly closed, and the ghostly stillness of the town could not be due solely to the hour. Traps had been laid everywhere, and although each one was a mere pebble against the sea, I knew that Devlin was on his guard.

I had two calls to make before I went after Devlin. The first was to Market Street. I sent my troops away on the rampage, because here I wanted to be alone. I chose my spot, and played a melody such as I had never played before. It was a melody of childhood, of reconciliation, almost of prayer. And out they came. Was it them? They stood at my feet, but I could not tell them apart. More and more came out, but it was the first that stayed with me, and one in particular that kept rubbing its head against my boot. With my music, I could convey no facts—only feelings, otherwise I should have stood there till the next night.

But I had to move on. I ended my melody, and hurried to my second destination. The rats were spreading through the streets like a flood, and the noise was intense. Soon they would have covered the whole town, and word would reach Devlin that the war had begun. He would be waiting for me, but this time he would not escape me.

Like everyone else, Jenkins had closed his shutters. I again sent my troops away, and banged on the door.

"Jenkins!" I cried. "Open up! It's me, Robert! Open your door!"

The bolt was drawn and the door opened.

"Robert! What's happening?"

I stepped inside, and he closed the door behind me. He held a lighted taper, and the flames emphasized the fear in his face.

"I've raised an army," I said. "The town is doomed, and so is Devlin. You must come with me so that I can protect you."

"Robert, no!" he cried. "Not the town! Devlin, yes, but not the whole town!"

"They don't deserve to survive," I said. "I shall give this town to my people."

"Robert, there's women, children . . . you can't do this."

"Do your people weep for mine?"

"What do you mean?"

"When my father was killed, did your people shed tears for me? Yours can't even shed tears for their own. You heard them cheer when the flames went up."

"Robert, you're a man now. These are your own kind."

"No, they're not my kind. I'm man and rat."

"You've condemned this town because of the way they killed Amadea. But what you're doing is worse even than their crime. They killed for ignorance, and you're killing for hate. That's not half rat, Robert. That's half man and half devil. Even rats don't kill for hate."

"Jenkins, I've come to save you. But if you want to stay, then stay."

While we talked, I had been removing my coachman's clothes, and now I began to put on the torn, bloodstained soldier's uniform that I had brought with me. I answered his unspoken question:

"Just a precaution. In case Devlin does something unexpected."

"Robert, I beg of you, be merciful to this town. Believe me, the people are not all evil. Devlin is not typical. There are kind people here, and innocent people."

"Jenkins," I said, "this world is ruled by men. What they like they keep, what they hate they destroy. Men rule because of their intelligence—that's what makes them king of the beasts, as you say. And if dogs had the brains of men, and men the brains of dogs, then dogs would rule, and they would kill what *they* hated. And their good would be the world's good, their bad the world's bad. You call rats vermin, and so you kill them.

Well I call men vermin, and if I rule, then I am right. That's the lesson men teach, and I abide by it. You have no exclusive claim on judgement. He who rules judges, and the code changes according to the ruler. In this town, rats are good and men are bad."

I was ready to leave now, but he stood against the door and barred my way.

"No, Robert," he said. "I can't let you do this. If you want to leave here, you'll have to kill me."

"When I leave here," I said, "I shall go for Devlin. But my presence or absence makes no difference to the town—it's already doomed. The rats are here, Jenkins. They won't go away. My concern now is only with Devlin."

"What will happen afterwards?"

"I haven't thought about afterwards. Perhaps I shall stay in the Palace."

"Could you lead the rats away again?"

"They'll obey me, if that's what you mean. Now let me pass, Jenkins. And if you won't come with me, then stay within doors. I still love you as a brother."

He stepped aside to let me pass.

"Robert," he said, "Devlin is dangerous. If he kills you, then no-one can save us. Be careful."

He opened the door. For a moment I wondered if perhaps he would strike me from behind to try and stop me, but he made no move.

The rats were crowding outside the door, but I summoned them away with a melody of war, and they left Jenkins alone. I went to the stables of the house next door, but the horses were already dead. Once again, I was obliged to walk, and the lost time was an irritant. It seemed to me that there was nothing Devlin could do, but the less time I gave him, the more sure was my success. Supposing he had run away, how would I find him? Where would he run to? It was doubtful that he would come into the town, and he would not risk the road we had taken together since my army might be there. But there were other routes. And the longer it took me to reach him, the more chance he would have of escape. I would find him, though. He knew I would hunt till I found him. He would not run away. He must not run away. He must stay and fight me to the end this time.

The doubts drove me faster through the streets, and the constant shrilling and rumbling rubbed at my nerves. I wished I had gone straight to the Palace. It had been a mistake to seek out the past when the present was so urgent and uncertain. Jenkins had disturbed me, too. I had counted on his support, but instead he had become a stranger.

There was a reddish glow in the sky. The sun did not rise over the river, and yet a sunrise light was coming from over there. Nothing seemed to be right any more. This was to be my day of triumph, but Jenkins had tarnished it, I had fears concerning Devlin's willingness to fight, and now the world had turned upside down and the sun rose in the west! If only I had had a horse, perhaps I would have been less irritable. I should have saved a horse instead of trying to save Jenkins.

The glow from the river was not the sunrise. It was the bridge. Devlin's men had set fire to it.

XXVI

My rats could go no further: the flames were too fierce and the water too swift. On the other side of the river I could see hundreds of men massed on the bank and on the road, all carrying lighted torches. Whichever direction we had come from, they would have met us with fire. It was a tactic I had not even considered, and yet I should have known for myself that fire was a weapon my army could not fight against.

No sooner had I consoled myself that we had at least captured the town than I caught sight of a mass of flames moving along the river bank towards us. More soldiers—scores of them—advancing many deep towards the squealing columns of my army. My rats had no choice but to press back into the town, and in the narrow street they met head on with their fellows pushing forward to the river. The soldiers came on, their torches held low in front of them. The slaughter must have been terrible judging from the noise and the sickly smell of burnt hair and flesh. But in the meantime, I had raced away down the bank and watched the scene clinging to reeds, my body half in and half out of the water.

I could do nothing to save my troops, but I knew that no matter how many were burnt, the vast majority would escape and would still hold the town in terror. Even now, I could see that the soldiers were being called back from the pursuit. Fire in such narrow streets could be even more catastrophic for the inhabitants than for the invaders.

Now my concern was to get across the river. Keeping close to the side, I waded further and further away from the bridge and the glow of the fire. I hoped that I might find a boat, but clearly these had all been taken across. My only other chance now was to swim. Could I risk the current? The alternative was to leave Devlin in command. And what other tricks might Devlin have in reserve? I must stop him, and what better time than now? He had ridden through the day with me, and then through the night, and then he would have spent yesterday setting up his defences . . . Even this night he would have spent organizing his men, and waiting for the attack. I had slept, but could he have slept? For all the power of his brain, he was weak in body. I must get to him before he could regain his strength. If he had hoped for respite now, he would be disappointed. I was cornered, and so I must attack.

I struck out across the river. The current took me even further downstream, but I was angry and desperate, and the thought of Devlin victorious took me to the other side. There I rested for a few moments, then I took out my sword and inflicted a few minor wounds upon myself. With blood and dirt on my face, and my soldier's uniform clinging in tatters to my bleeding body, I went to the road, and began a staggering walk towards the burning bridge. I took just one risk, hiding my recorder at my back, between trousers and tunic. Otherwise, I retained not a vestige of the Coachman Rat.

"Hey, who's that?" came a cry.

"Help me! Help me!" I shouted.

Some soldiers came running towards me.

"He's hurt," said one.

"Where'd you come from?" asked another.

"Devlin sent us!" I gasped. "Scouting party . . . The others are dead!"

"The scouting party! We thought you'd all been killed!"

"I got away. Where's Mr. Devlin?"

"He'll be at the Palace. Is anything coming this way?"

"Rats, you mean?"

"Rats, and the Coachman."

"I can't tell you that. I have to see Mr. Devlin first."

"You'd better get those wounds seen to as well. Come on, we'll get you back."

"No, no, you'll be needed here. Just give me a horse, and I'll make my own way back."

"All right if you think you can manage."

They helped me up on to a horse, and off I rode to the Palace. The light was stronger now, but I had no fear of being recognized in this disguise. I reached the steps, and staged a painful dismount from the horse, in keeping with the wounds I appeared to have suffered. There were just two guards outside the golden gate, and one of them came down the steps to investigate.

"Amadeus, scouting party," I said. "I've got to see Mr. Devlin!"

"We thought you were all dead!" said the guard.

"The others are," I said. "But I got away. You'd better take me to Mr. Devlin."

"He gave orders he's not to be disturbed except in an emergency."

"This is an emergency, man! With wounds like these you don't think I'd come here otherwise, do you?"

The guard looked and nodded, then he accompanied me up the steps.

"From the scouting party," he told his colleague. "Wants to see Mr. Devlin."

He knocked and the golden door was opened from the inside.

"Survivor from the scouting party," he said. "Says he's got to see Mr. Devlin."

There was only the one guard on the inside. He closed the door behind me.

"You'd better give me the message," he said. "Mr. Devlin'll be resting now."

"Mr. Devlin said I was to report to him personally," I said.

"Mr. Devlin thinks you're dead."

"If you don't get me to him soon, that's what I shall be. Can't you see this is an emergency?"

The urgency of the tone, and the freshness of the blood finally convinced him. He began to accompany me up the stairs.

"I know where he is," I said. "You must stay at your post. You can't leave the door unmanned."

There was another guard outside Devlin's apartment. Once more I had to tell my story and show my wounds, but this man was adamant that Devlin was not to be woken. He had explicit instructions. I would have to wait.

"All right," I said. "Just see if he's asleep now, and if he is, I'll wait."

The guard saw the sense in this, and turned to open the door. As he turned, I drew my sword and ran him through. I pushed his body into the room, closed the door behind me, and walked through to Devlin's bedroom.

Everything was exactly as before: the day was breaking, Devlin was asleep, and I was standing over him in total command. It seemed absurd to be repeating a scene that had taken place only two days before, but the absurdity was something that Devlin did not appreciate. I awakened him by putting my hand over his nose and mouth, so that he could not breathe.

His eyes opened wide in terror, and then began to bulge. His face had turned purple before I finally removed my hand. He gasped for air.

"This time you won't escape," I said.

"Guard!" he screamed, and tried to leap out of the bed. I held him down.

"The guard is dead," I said. "And those at the gate won't hear you."

He lay still for a moment looking up at me with fear-drawn eyes.

"Get it over with," he said.

"Not yet," I said. "I need something from you. A document. I'm going to take control of your army."

The eyes flickered, and the expression indicated that the brain had taken over from the heart.

"How did you get through?" he asked. "I stationed troops everywhere."

"Get up," I said.

Keeping his eyes on me all the time, he eased himself out of the bed.

"You tricked them with the uniform, I suppose," he said. "I underestimated you."

"Go to your writing-table."

"Listen," he said. "There's no reason for us to fight each other. We can rule this town together . . ."

"Sit down."

He sat.

"In many ways," he said, "our talents complement each other. We can come to an underst . . ."

"Take pen and paper, and write what I tell you."

He looked hard at me, then smiled.

"I shan't write your letter," he said. "If that's what you need, then that's my escape route to life. You won't kill me until you have it. And so I shan't let you have it."

I swung the sword, and it sliced into the flesh of his upper left arm. He screamed, and clutched the wound as the blood poured out over his nightshirt.

"Take pen and paper," I said, "and write what I tell you."

His face was ash-grey, and he had doubled over with pain and fear, but the voice still emerged with defiance:

"You'll have to kill me, then."

I swung the sword again, and it cut into his left thigh. Again he screamed, but still he would not write.

"Does life mean so much to you, then?" I said. "All right, Devlin, you can have your life. Write the letter, and I'll leave you here. Once I have the letter, it won't matter to me whether you live or die, because you can't stop me."

He ceased groaning, and painfully raised his head.

"I can't trust you," he said.

"You have no choice," I said. "If you don't give me the letter, I shall kill you. If you do, I shall leave you here. You may bleed to death, of course, but at least you'll have a chance. But I'll make a condition for sparing you."

Despite the pain, the eyes flickered again as the brain took over.

"What condition?"

"That you stay in the Palace. Make no attempt to leave here. I don't want you staggering to the river and revoking the letter."

I could almost have laughed, seeing the hope and the cunning resume in those eyes.

"I'll give you my word on that," he said.

"If you break your word, I'll kill you," I said.

"I swear to you I shan't leave this Palace," he said.

"Very well. Take your pen and paper."

He did so.

"I presume John is in command during your absence?"

He nodded.

"Dear John, obey whatever instructions Private Amadeus gives you."

"Amadeus?" Devlin paused over the name.

"Why not?" I said. Write."

He wrote.

"He has escaped from the coachman, and knows his plans. I will join you shortly. Signed Devlin."

He finished writing.

"There's blood on it," he said.

"I'll say it's mine."

He had written the letter as I had dictated it. I took it from him.

"You realize this is the death warrant for a thousand men," I said

"You gave me no choice," he said. "Their lives or mine."

"Keep your word," I said, and left him. I stepped over the dead body of the guard, closed Devlin's door behind me, and then waited in the passage outside.

I could hear Devlin moving about and groaning. The wounds were severe, but he would not die from them. Both he and I knew that. And both he and I knew what he would do next.

The door opened. He had managed to dress himself, and now out he came into the passage, only to find me standing in front of him, with sword upraised.

"Words are only words," I said.

And I cut him down.

XXVII

It gave me no satisfaction to kill Devlin. But I felt no pity for him either. He was a fragile, dead man lying in a pool of blood, and he was nothing more.

I sheathed my sword, and went downstairs.

"Everything all right?" asked the guard at the door.

"You're to come with me," I said. "You and the others."

I showed him Devlin's letter.

"What's happening, then?" he asked. "Where's Mr. Devlin?"

"He's still resting," I said, "after his ordeal. The other guard'll look after him. I'm going to need every man I can get. The Coachman's going to mount a big attack on the town, but I know how we can beat him. Where's the coach that Mr. Devlin drove here?"

"In the stables."

"Come on, then. We've no time to lose."

He opened the door. I ordered the other two guards to hitch up the horses and accompany me as well, and they all got in the coach, which I then drove at furious pace to the river. Regaining my coach gave me considerably more satisfaction than killing Devlin.

"Where's Captain John?" I shouted to a group of soldiers near the bridge.

They gave me directions. I called out to the guards inside the coach to get out and join the others, which they did. Then I drove on to a tent that had been pitched on the river bank itself, upstream of the bridge. By now it was daylight, and I wondered if my disguise would deceive John. He had often seen me at the Palace, and if he were to recognize me now, it would mean my certain death. I pulled my cap well down over my eyes, and jumped down.

"Where's Captain John?" I asked in a tone of utmost urgency.

"In the tent. What do you want?" asked the soldier I had spoken to.

"I've got to see him quickly. Here, show him this."

The soldier took Devlin's letter inside, and a moment later John came out.

"Are you Amadeus?" he asked.

"Yes, sir," I said.

"He's the one who was in the scouting party," said the soldier, who had evidently been told of my arrival earlier.

"There was no Amadeus in the scouting party," said John, frowning. "An Ambrose . . ."

"Ambrose was sick and couldn't go, sir. I took his place. Sir, there is no time to lose."

"Where's Mr. Devlin?"

"Mr. Devlin is exhausted, sir. He'll come soon, when he's rested, but you must remember that he's had no sleep for two days and two nights. Sir, if we stay here talking, we shall be too late."

John was no general. He had been put in charge of the army because Devlin knew he could trust him and dominate him. This was my good fortune.

"What's going on, then?" he asked.

"The Coachman plans a second wave of attacks on the town, coming from the east," I said. "The first lot that your men beat back over there was nothing—just the advance guard. The Coachman himself will be leading the main force, and we've got to get all our men across to the other side if we're going to stand a chance."

"You mean he's not taking this road?"

"He got his whole army across the river miles back along the road. Have you got boats here?"

"Yes, we've got boats."

"Then for heaven's sake, get your men across the river. And I shall need my coach and horses over there, too."

"The coach and horses?"

"How else am I going to be able to move fast enough? Think, man. The Coachman's descending on this town with about a million rats. He's going to attack us on all fronts. I've got to be mobile to co-ordinate our defence. Now if you'll start getting the men across, I'll explain my plan to you as we go."

He gave the order, and soon the soldiers were being ferried across the river in boatloads. The coach and horses presented a problem which I had to solve for the captain. I had the men rope two boats together for the coach, and we unhitched the horses so that they could be transported separately. In the meantime, I had ordered that all the torches were to be doused and left behind.

"Fire is the last thing we want," I explained to John. "For one thing, we could set the whole town alight, and for another, the soldiers will need both hands free for fighting."

As we rowed across the river, I explained my plan to John.

"The vital thing," I said, "is that we should be in position before they attack. That's why we've got to move fast. I aim to station our men in detachments of fifty to a hundred at various key points in the town. Now those key points will be the narrow streets that our men can block by themselves. The rats have to go down those streets, and once they're advancing they can't retreat, because of the rats behind, right? Now our men have two weapons that the rats can't combat—swords and boots. When the rats approach, our men will march. They won't kill everything, but if the timing is right, they'll kill a lot. We'll decimate the enemy."

"Sounds all right to me," said John. "What about the Coachman himself? Mr. Devlin wanted him caught or killed."

"We'll catch him all right," I said. "You and I will see to him."

We had reached the other side of the river. My horses were hitched up to the coach again, and I told John to get all his men together. Those who had originally been on this side of the river were now to douse their torches, and dispose of them.

The strategy was simple. I would split this army up into small groups, trap them in narrow alleyways, and then set my hordes on them one group at a time. The problem was to place the groups far enough apart to prevent them linking up again. I estimated that there were about a thousand men all told, and this meant fifteen to twenty groups at different points in the town.

Eventually, we had divided them, and now I stood on my coach with Captain John at my side.

"Will you address them, sir, or shall I?" I asked.

"You'd better do it," he said.

"Listen, men!" I cried. "We're going to enter the town. At various intervals, we shall leave behind one detachment, then another, so that we shall have you deployed at all the key positions in the town. Once you are in position, you are to wait in absolute silence. When the rats enter your sector, your first advantage will be surprise. Your second will be sheer weight. You will march towards them, they'll be unable to retreat, and as far as you're concerned, it'll be like treading on a thick carpet. But use your swords as well as your feet. Captain John and I will be driving round to co-ordinate the defence. Until the rats arrive, be vigilant. You'll hear them when they come. And when they do come, you march! I hope nobody's squeamish at the sight of rats' blood."

There was laughter from the men.

"We're ready to go now, sir," I said to Captain John.

"I must own to you," he said, "I've not had much experience o' this sort o' thing. I'd best leave it in your hands."

He and I rode at the head of the troops, and whenever we reached a suitable alleyway, we would leave behind one of our detachments. By now, there were plenty of ordinary citizens emerging from the houses, and John asked me if they should be told to stay inside.

"Not necessary," I said. "They'll hear when the rats come, and then they must take shelter for themselves."

"One thing I have noticed," said John. "There's no rats in the streets at all."

"As I told you, the main force is still on its way. Your men must have killed most of the advance guard."

He looked pleased. How is a palace guard to know that rats hunt by night? Would even a real captain know that the last place a rat would enter in the day is a street occupied by a thousand soldiers? But I knew where my army was. They were hiding away in the sewers, the gardens, the yards, the buildings, the dumps, the shadows, the crannies. They were gathering strength after the long march and the night attack.

By midday, the soldiers were all in position. John and I drove round and round, ostensibly to check, and to 'co-ordinate', but in reality for me to memorize the exact position of each detachment.

The day wore on. With each visit, we found the soldiers more and more restless. "When are they coming?" was the question they kept asking, but even that began to change by evening to: "Are they coming?" Several soldiers did point out that rats were creatures of the night, and I would then nod agreement and say they might well attack only when it was dark, but we could not be sure and so we must be prepared for all eventualities.

"I wish Mr. Devlin would come," said John.

But as the sun began to set, there was no more sign of Mr. Devlin than there was of the army of rats and their leader.

"Before night comes," I said to John, "I think we should drive to the eastern hill, to see if there's anything approaching. My guess is that they'll be within sight now."

He readily agreed, and so I drove out of the town with him, and up to the top of the hill. Dusk was now falling fast. We stood up, and both scanned the horizon.

"Look! Over there!" I said. "The darkness in the fields."

He strained his eyes to penetrate the gloom.

"I can't see anything," he said.

"In the fields!" I repeated. "Like a moving black shadow!"

He was totally absorbed in his search for the moving black shadow, and can have felt scarcely any pain as my sword slid between his ribs and found his heart. It was a merciful death compared with that which awaited his fellow-soldiers.

XXVIII

I drove back into the town. The citizens had already locked themselves away behind doors and shutters, so evidently word had gone round about the impending battle. I summoned my troops. It must have been an eerie sound from afar—the sound of a recorder playing through the night air.

Out came the rats. I kept well away from the soldier-packed alleys, and as I drove and summoned, so my army swelled, and the rustling and whistling grew ever louder and ever more menacing. They came from all directions, and I had to go slowly to avoid crushing them with hooves or wheels. Follow, follow, called the recorder, and the night echoed with the answers of the followers.

We closed in on the first detachment. I changed the tone from summons to attack, and sent them racing in from both ends of the street.

"March!" came a desperate cry, but where could they march to? When one stopped, all had to stop, and the teeth tore at them from before and behind. If they swung their swords, they were more likely to strike each other than strike a rat, and in the darkness they were fighting an almost invisible enemy anyway. They hadn't a chance. The rumbling feet and screeching voices of my army were punctuated by the agonized screams of

154

Devlin's soldiers, as one by one they fell beneath the unending onslaught. Wave upon wave of rats ripped them apart.

I shall not dwell upon the battle. Systematically my soldiers destroyed Devlin's. I had placed each group of men at some distance from the next, so that they could not know the outcome of the previous encounter. We simply moved from one section to another, gathering reinforcements as we went, and the night had barely reached its darkest when the last of the detachments was wiped out. In a few short hours we had killed a thousand men.

Why did they not realize the hopelessness of their position? Why did they not run from the trap I had put them in? Afterwards, when my army had dispersed to plunder their town, and when I sat in the driving-seat of my coach, looking down the dark alleyways of the last slaughter, I pondered long on this question. It seemed to me that the soldiers had acquiesced in their own death, just as the mob had accepted the death of the Prince and Amadea. True, the soldiers had fought against my rats, but why had they not fought against the need to fight? There was a weakness in this monster that ruled the world—a strange deficiency that made him accept even his own exposure to destruction. Gradually the nature of the deficiency became clear to me: it was his reliance on his fellow man.

Sooner or later, inevitably, men would rely upon fools, devils, or lunatics. And if the time should ever come when whole continents relied on single rulers or governments, then men would follow the path to destruction of their whole species.

This thought made me neither joyful nor sad, but it was a thought that I wanted to share and discuss, and on an impulse I drove to Jenkins' lodging. Although it was still night, he was not in bed.

"How could I sleep, knowing what was going on? What's happened? Are the soldiers dead, or are you a fugitive?"

"The soldiers are dead," I said. "And so is Devlin. The town is ours now."

He slumped into a chair.

"Robert," he said, and I saw that he was weeping. "Robert, you're insane."

"Only because you see things as a human," I said. "You forget that I'm a rat."

"Since when a rat? You have a human body, a human heart, human culture, human speech! You turned your back on the rat species, you *wanted* to be human. You were given the form, and I helped to give you the soul. Since when are you a rat?"

"Since Devlin burned Amadea," I said. "And since I learned the truth about men?"

"What truth? What truth have you learned?"

I told him the thoughts I had had about man's dependence, about the inevitability of foolish or evil government, the lunatic ruler, the path to total destruction.

"There is no such thing as man," he said. "There are only men, women and children. And all are different, and if some follow, others will rebel and others will wait and others will judge. It's only the balance that changes."

"Sooner or later," I said, "the balance will always shift towards evil."

"That I will never believe," he said. "And history proves you wrong. But where do you stand in all this, Robert? You, who rule the rat army which follows your instructions just as Devlin's soldiers did. You've turned them into an obedient mob, and now you'll lead them to their destruction. Where's the difference between you and Devlin, you and the lunatic ruler?"

"I don't intend to rule," I said. "When we've finished conquering this town, I shall leave my rats to rule themselves, as they've always done."

"You're wrong on two counts," he said. "Wrong about yourself, and wrong about what you're doing for them. You believe you're conquering the town for their sake. But I told you before, the killing is not for love of them, it's for hate. You fell in love with Amadea, and now you want revenge. The rest is self-deception."

His words hurt. Jenkins always found words that struck deeply. But I denied them.

"I'm giving this town to rats," I said, "because man is unworthy of it. Rats have a better system of government, a better chance of survival, and they don't kill except in order to survive."

"You're the lunatic ruler, Robert. Killing out of revenge, deluding yourself about motives, and ultimately . . . do you know ultimately, Robert, where you'll lead your army? Straight to destruction. When you've finished killing everyone in this town, how long do you think your rats will survive? A month, two months, three? What do your rats feed off? Men! When the food runs short, they'll have no choice but to turn against each other. Maybe some will get away to the country, but the rest . . . led by their lunatic king to starvation and cannibalism."

I do not know how long I sat staring at him.

Yet again the world had been turned upside down. At length I managed to speak:

"Why didn't you tell me this before?"

"I didn't think of it before. I'm not a ruler, Robert. Why didn't *you* think of it?"

Why indeed? For I had known it all my life. But in my headlong pursuit of revenge, I had forgotten it.

"Jenkins, be a ruler. Rule this town with me. We can find a way for man and rat to live together—we can establish a balance."

"There *was* a balance. We survived, you survived. But you weren't satisfied. You wanted dominance."

"No," I said. "No, you were right. It wasn't for them, it was for revenge. If Devlin hadn't killed Amadea . . . Oh Jenkins, I saw paradise, and he destroyed it."

We sat in silence for a long time. I could not straighten out the confusion of my thoughts. More that anything, I wanted Jenkins to guide me and at length I simply asked him what I should do.

"Take them away," he said.

"Where to?" I asked. "If one follows, all follow. Where can I take such a multitude?"

"Take them to the other town," he said. "At least they still have cats and dogs to defend them."

"There'd be war," I said. "If my army won, I'd have the same problem as here. And if they lost . . . how can I lead them to that?"

"Then stay," he said. "We men are ingenious. And we also like to survive. We'll find ways. If there's food enough for them, your rats won't attack us, will they? Perhaps we'll learn to welcome them, share with them, live with them."

"They'll multiply," I said. "In my wisdom, I saw them multiply and dominate the earth. And I forgot that they would have to eat."

"As I said, some will go to the country."

"Town rats need men. Besides, who sows the seeds? They'll multiply till you'll be forced to wage war on them. I've brought too many."

"Then leave us to wage war on them. Their survival depends on ours, so leave us to think out our survival strategy. And don't interfere if we have to cull them."

The solution, then, was for me to withdraw. Without me, the townspeople would find means of redressing the balance that I had ruined. Men would resume dominance, and rats would feed off them as before. But many would have to die.

"I don't want them to die," I said. "I didn't bring them here to die. How can I be at peace with myself?"

"Close your eyes," he said. "Pretend nothing is happening. It's a common human trick. When we're disturbed, we turn away and gaze elsewhere. That's a survival strategy, too—otherwise, who would ever stop thinking about his death?"

"I can't close my eyes," I said.

"Then go where you can't see. Leave this town."

But I could never have done that either. How could I have lived on, not knowing what had happened? I could understand the necessity of my keeping away, but *I* had to survive, too, and so long as I survived I had to bear my own company, and my own thoughts.

Jenkins found the solution. He proposed that I should stay in the Palace. With the burning of the bridge, the rats could not get across the river, but he would still be able to come and visit me and report to me on what was happening. I would have to be strong-willed, and resist the temptation to row across myself, because—as he said—there was no telling what effect my presence might have both on rats and on people.

There was in fact an urgent reason for going to the Palace right away. Dr. Richter was amongst the prisoners in the dungeon, and Jenkins wanted to free him. He thought that Dr. Richter and some of the other prominent prisoners might help to co-ordinate work in the town.

"I know you have mixed feelings about Dr. Richter," he said, "but he is a fine man and a good organizer."

I did not doubt Jenkins' judgement. We were about to leave when he put his hand on my shoulder.

"Robert, what you have done is terrible beyond words. I can no more condone your violence than I could condone Devlin's. But there are other things that should not remain unsaid. You've saved this town from a real tyrant. And the thousand soldiers you killed were the heel with which Devlin would have crushed the people. I'll try to make this known. And I want to say also that I'm grateful for your friendship."

We embraced, and I felt that a shadow had lifted from me. I was, perhaps, just another step in my humanization. I was no longer isolated, and no longer responsible. I could now depend on Jenkins.

XXIX

I duly took up residence in the Palace. I could have had any rooms I liked, but those associated with Amadea made me weep, and those associated with Devlin were repugnant; I therefore went back to the tiny room I had occupied before. There was no-one else in the Palace except the domestic staff, for the prisoners were all released, and the guards and soldiers were all dead. I was now Prince, but with no Princess, no duties, no people.

Jenkins came to see me every day. His visits were all that I had to look forward to. He told me that life was slowly returning to normal after the violent upheavals that had recently racked the town. In the early days, there were frequent cases of people being attacked by rats, the very young and the very old being particularly vulnerable. Jenkins' theory was that some rats must have developed a taste for human meat after the ferocious attack on Devlin's soldiers. Rats were hunting even by day, no doubt emboldened by the absence of cats and dogs, and perhaps driven also by the competition for food that must have resulted from their enormous numbers. However, the frequency of these cases slowly dwindled when traps of poisoned meat were laid. Jenkins did not want to tell me about these, but I insisted on being told of all measures that were taken.

It also transpired that quite a number of cats and dogs had been hidden away by their owners, and once it became apparent that Richter and his colleagues *wanted* these animals to be let loose on the streets, the old enemy began to reappear. Some enterprising merchants actually journeyed to neighbouring towns to bring back kittens and puppies, which they sold at considerable profit to themselves though claiming and achieving recognition as public benefactors.

I kept to my agreement with Jenkins, and never once left the confines of the Palace and its gardens. The domestic staff served me, but afforded me no companionship. The girl that I had kissed had left to get married, and the remainder were mainly old and mechanical. They would respond minimally to my attempts at conversation, and were plainly anxious to go about their business away from me. Perhaps they were more sociable with one another, but certainly in my presence they were unyielding.

Thus I divided my days between meals and walks,

books and thoughts, all experienced in isolation. Only the visits from Jenkins provided a link with the real world. One day, I begged him to let me go back to the town with him.

"Soon," he promised. "But rats are still dying in the streets. It's better for you not to see."

"I thought the poisoning had finished," I said.

"We thought so, too. But it seems that some citizens have taken the law into their own hands. There have been a lot of cases recently. And whoever's responsible has learnt his lesson from you—no trace of culprit or poison. We'll stop it eventually, but it's not an easy task. You must trust me, Robert—I'll take you back when it's safe for you and for the town. In the meantime, wait in patience."

He did not come again for several days, and the strain on my patience was becoming intolerable. I sent one of the servants into town to find out what was happening. He returned with news that someone had been poisoning not only rats but also people, and there was a great deal of fear and suspicion everywhere.

"There are those, Sir," he said, not without a ring of hostility, "that say it be the Coachman."

"How can it be me?" I snapped. "I've never left the Palace."

"Some talk of witchcraft," he said. "You don't need to leave the Palace to do witchcraft. Though 'tis only what they say, Sir. I can only report what they say."

"Did you talk to Mr. Jenkins?"

"He weren't at his home, Sir."

"Then who did you speak to?"

"Just people, Sir. Ordinary people. Might I get on with my work now, Sir?"

Was it to start all over again? Was another Devlin about to lead a mob to the Palace and set me up on a pile of firewood? Surely not Jenkins. But why not Jenkins? Was not Jenkins as faithful a member of the monster species as Devlin? Could any of them be trusted? Someone was murdering rats and people. If Richter and Jenkins could find a victim to blame, then the ruled would go on accepting their rulers. But if no poisoner was found, then the scene would be set for a new ruler to rise. What better victim than the coachman rat, the legendary slayer of animals and men?

But if they killed me, the poisoning would still go on. They must know that. No, they would not know that. They would believe I was guilty, and would go on believing it till events proved them wrong. And Jenkins—whom I depended on—believed it like the rest. Why else had he stayed away from me?

From this moment on, I would eat none of the food prepared for me. I made my own meals, I never walked save with a sword in my hand. I slept behind locked doors and always uneasily, listening for the stealthy movement in the dark. For three days and three nights I waited for the false justice. But no-one came. Why were they waiting? If the murderer had been found, why didn't Jenkins come? And one more question, without influence on my safety, and yet as haunting as the rest: Who would want to poison rats and men together? Who could have, and why could he have so much hatred for the two species?

The answer to these questions came unexpectedly one afternoon. There was a knock at my door. I seized my sword and demanded to know who it was.

"Jenkins!" came the reply. "I've got Dr. Richter with me."

"Who else?" I asked.

"No-one," he said. "Robert, let us in."

Keeping my sword in my hand, I unlocked the door.

At once I knew that I had nothing to fear from them, for on their faces were deep grooves of worry, and they had come for need and not for hate.

"What's the matter?" I asked.

"May we sit down?" asked Dr. Richter.

He looked even older than when I had first seen him. The grey hair was loose and untidy, and the hand that held the walking stick was trembling slightly. When he sat down, it was almost as if he lost control of his body—he fell rather than sat.

Jenkins, too, looked sickly. There were dark rings under his eyes, and I fancied that he was also trembling slightly. Clearly he had terrible news to give me, and was not sure how to fashion it.

"There's something wrong," I said. "You've come to tell me, so tell me."

"Robert," said Jenkins. "I came to see you several days ago, and I told you that the rats were being secretly poisoned."

"I've heard more since," I told him. "I know that men are being poisoned too."

"Yes," he said. "Rats and men, dying by the score. Dr. Richter and I have been working night and day, Robert, and now we've discovered the cause of these deaths. No poison, no murderer."

"What then?"

"Robert, they're dying of the plague."

The word was like a withered hand reaching out to clutch the heart. Plague. I had read how whole towns had been wiped out, and there was no known cure. The carriers? My rats. The victims? Rats and men alike. Now they would all perish in a paroxysm of destruction that neither I nor Richter nor any ruler in the land could control.

"Could you be wrong?" I asked.

"No," said Dr. Richter, "there's no mistaking the signs now."

"Then we're still doomed," I said. "Rats and men, we'll die together."

"Not all," said Dr. Richter. "There's a way of saving a great number of people still."

"What way?" I asked.

They looked at each other. Dr. Richter nodded, and it was Jenkins who spoke now:

"It's you who can save them, Robert. The disease is carried by fleas that feed on rats. If we can destroy the rats, we'll destroy the fleas. And so we've come to ask you if you'll help us."

"You want me to kill rats?"

"Either the rats die, or rats and humans die. There's no way to save the rats, Robert. But we *can* save people."

"Even if I agreed," I said, "there's no way that I could kill *all* my rats. You'd need a palace full of poison."

"We need no poison," said Jenkins. "We want you to go through the town with your recorder and get them to follow you. And then lead them to the river, and drown them."

XXX

I knew what they wanted. I had read the history book. But I wanted to close my eyes, and even now I wanted not to know.

165

"You're asking me to commit genocide!" I cried.

"You have already," said Dr. Richter quietly. "It was you who brought them there."

Jenkins laid his hand gently on my arm.

"Robert," he said, "if the Prince and Amadea had been alive now, and *they* had asked you to do this thing for them, in the name of your own humanity, would you have refused them?"

I could not answer him. Instead, I asked him and Dr. Richter to leave me alone for a few minutes. They went out without another word.

I fell to my knees. My sword was within reach, and for a moment I imagined taking it and ending my misery. But I knew that it would not end. My misery was the plague, and the plague would claim its victims regardless of my death.

"Oh help me!" I cried, and with all the strength of my spirit I sought to summon the woman of light to me. She alone had the power to end the agony. She could touch the town, and cleanse it. Me she could touch, and give me peace.

But she did not come. It had to be my decision. Alone again, responsible again, burdened now with the last function I would ever have wanted. But Jenkins was right. Jenkins was always right. Had Amadea asked me to do it, I would have known that there was no choice, and in truth what choice was there? Stand and watch Jenkins, Dr. Richter, and the rest, and myself—all swell, darken and die? And the rats would die anyway.

With my recorder in my hand, I joined Jenkins and Dr. Richter outside, and we left the Palace, made our way to the river, and stepped into a waiting boat.

"It seems there's never to be peace in this life," I said. "Every journey leads to a different nightmare."

"Nightmares," said Dr. Richter, "end when we wake."

"Are we asleep then?" asked Jenkins, but Dr. Richter did not reply.

On the way, we decided that I should wait till night to dance my rats to the water. The people meanwhile would be warned to stay indoors, although it was customary to do so anyway. I would ride in my coach, which had been kept for me in Dr. Richter's own stable, and when the slaughter was over, I would return to Dr. Richter's house, where Jenkins would also be staying.

Dr. Richter's coach was waiting for us on the other side of the river, and as we drove through town I saw the signs of the plague. There were dying rats in the roads, and there were black draped windows in many houses. And yet there were still people in the streets, still merchants selling wares, still men and women buying. A group of children were playing in an alleyway, and singing as they played.

"Are they not afraid?" I asked Jenkins.

"Only when they stop," he said.

We drove to the market-place and pulled up at the large building with the grand entrance of the clock. Here I had first come with Devlin, on the day of the betrayal. Dr. Richter led the way inside, not to the hall of that first meeting, but to a room on the ground floor. There were a number of serious-faced men at a table, and one or two of the faces were familiar to me—perhaps from Devlin's circle, perhaps from Dr. Richter's.

"Gentlemen," said Dr. Richter, "may I present to you the coachman, Robert? We have explained the situation to him, and he has agreed to our plan."

Spontaneously the men broke into applause. Then they stood, and some crowded round me to thank me.

"I've done nothing," I said. "And what I shall try to do is no cause for gratitude or for celebration. Whatever the outcome, we shall all be weeping tomorrow."

Plans were hastily made for informing the people of what was to be done. There were then discussions concerning treatment of the sick and burial of the dead, Jenkins and I sat at the table near Dr. Richter, but we took no part in these talks. I was impressed with the orderliness of the meeting, and with Dr. Richter's firm but fair control of the discussions. Jenkins had been right—as always—in his choice of leader.

"If there's nothing more to be said," announced Dr. Richter finally, "then I'll close the meeting."

"There is one thing more," I intervened. There was immediate attentiveness from everyone present. "I wish to make a condition for what I'm about to do."

"Anything," said Dr. Richter. "Our debt to you is already beyond payment."

"Regardless of failure or success, I want a monument to be built. There is a hill overlooking this city, and in the earth of that hill lie the bodies of the Prince and Amadea. I want a monument of gold to be built on that hill."

"It shall be done," said Dr. Richter.

He then drove Jenkins and myself to his home, and there we waited until nightfall.

How am I to describe the events of that night? Where are the words that could make real the horror of what I did? For you who read my story, this was the destruction of vermin, because you feel for no other form of life but your own. For me they were kin, my own species. I had sprung from them, lived with them, fought alongside them. And now they had put their trust in me, but ten times more treacherously than a Devlin, I led them to annihilation.

Let me narrate the mere facts. With my own coach and horses I drove all through the town, summoning my rats from every quarter. For all the deaths, it was a mighty army, and the whole world seemed to shake as if

Venus had descended again to overturn it. I took them down to the river. The only light was from the full moon, beneath which the water flashed and glinted as it went racing by. I made my horses wade into the flood until their very haunches were submerged. They were strong enough and, with the coach, heavy enough to resist the currents. Then I stood on the roof, and played melodies that promised unending bliss to those that followed me. And into the water they poured, like molten lava in a ceaseless flow, thence to be swept away by the remorseless surge. The squeals of terror were the arrows they fired into me, but I played on, and on they came. A few managed to reach the coach and clamber on to the roof with me. They did not attack me. They crouched at my feet, as if being there were some rich reward. But the rest were pulled away, swimming, struggling, until the river sucked them down into its capacious depths.

Through my own tears I played on and on until the realization came to me that I was playing in total silence. The only accompaniment to my songs was the rushing of the water. I stopped. Was ever a night so heavy with death?

I sank to my knees, and played one last tune. This was a tune of sorrow, of heartstrings breaking, of eternal farewells. It sang of the lost world and the nevermore. I wanted it to be my own death-song, but I could not die. My spirit longed to depart, but my body held it back, allowing only the musical notes to fly away into the laden night.

When the song was over, I threw my recorder into the water, and watched it leap away as if glad to be freed. The rats on the roof were dead, and when I looked to the front of my coach, I could only just make out the tops of my horses' heads. They, too, were dead, their slumped bodies held up by the harness. At that moment

I was the only creature in the universe. I was Atlas, but wilting beneath the weight. I was the Angel of Death. I was the beginning and the end.

"Change me back!" I cried. "Oh, for pity, change me back!"

XXXI

Let us be done with my story. I returned on foot to Dr. Richter's house. Here I demanded and was given a coach and a team of horses. Dr. Richter and Jenkins begged me to stay with them, but I could not bear their company or that of the townspeople who had congregated in the streets to give thanks. Thanks for what? I had saved no-one. They would all die another day.

I rode and rode, stopping only to rest my horses, and never for one moment was I free from the sound of my recorder and the terror of my dying people. I crossed plains and mountains, villages and towns, until one day I became feverish. Some kindly country folk transported me the house of a Dr. J. Erasmus. Soon swellings began to appear beneath my arms, in my groin, at the sides of my neck. Strange patches darkened my skin. I have the plague, and shortly I shall be dead. I am glad. Were it not for the pain, I should be only thankful—and yet even the pain I welcome, because it is a merited punishment.

I have begged Dr. Erasmus to write down my story, as I can no longer hold a pen myself. He has rebuked me for my despair, but I am not in despair. I do not want to live because life can only be a torment to me. In death I hope to be united with the woman of light and Amadea, whom I shall love for ever.

Dr. Erasmus asks me to end with a message of encouragement for the living, but my story has nothing encouraging or discouraging to offer. What happened, happened, and was itself for good or bad. I have no message to give. He asks me at least to say I love my fellow man, but I can think only that I killed my fellow rat. Perhaps the good doctor does not understand that I am different . . .